Pra...

SUGAR STREET

"[*Sugar Street*'s narrator] is looking not merely to escape, he tells us, but to disappear completely—to murder his former self and live out his remaining days as someone else . . . it's in the methodical unpacking of how a human being might effectively cease to exist without actually committing suicide that *Sugar Street* is at its most enthralling."
—New York Times Book Review

"Clean, raw, terse . . . perfectly paced . . . You sure won't see the ending coming." **—Financial Times**

"A fast, daring, completely original book, with one of the smartest and most surprising (yet perfect) endings in recent memory. Dee presents as an American Dostoevsky, offering strange, rich insights." **—Esquire**

"A bravura exercise in generating suspense with relatively limited means . . . The stage is set for a propulsive post-heist thriller, with inbuilt tension, in the sense that the narrator will be rumbled before long—but for what? While key disclosures are expertly postponed, we soon sense that *Sugar Street* hunts bigger game in any case, with the getaway premise only a pretext for exploring nothing less than the politics of 21st-century selfhood." **—The Guardian (UK)**

"*Sugar Street* is expertly done, with a good balance of provocative thinking and surprising developments, remaining satisfying even when we can see that the seeds of the ominous ending were planted early on, right in the structure of the man's life and maybe even in society itself. At times I wanted it to work out its themes more explicitly, but then again, no. Leave space for the reader to think—after all, too much extraneous babble, especially online, is one of the things the narrator stands against." **—The Times** (UK)

"[*Sugar Street*'s] narrator, to an ultimately devastating degree, is unpredictable . . . Dee is skilled at creating and examining multifaceted tension on the page, sustaining it as his narrator, who hurls contempt at most of the things around him, takes on the very qualities he deems contemptible."
—Minneapolis Star Tribune

"A fantastic subversion of an old American story . . . Just as satire can critique through its comedic exaggeration in representing systems of power, misanthropy in the novel can critique contemporary injustices through its ecstatic delivery of its barbs. This is what Dee has tapped into with *Sugar Street*: an entertaining and enlivening cynicism that belongs to the tradition of Celine, Bernhard, Gaddis, Williams."
—Electric Literature

"An energetic character study of a white man determined to escape from his life . . . Dee's work grapples intriguingly with the narrator's liberal myopia. It stands as a showcase of Dee's masterly prose." —*Publishers Weekly*

"An unsettling, propulsive, sometimes acidly funny book." —*Kirkus Reviews*

"A story of the desperation and ultimate impossibility of isolation, Dee's narrative is a spider web of questions that won't let readers go, questions like where does insanity begin and end? Readers of Dee's earlier novels will not want to miss this page-turner." —*Library Journal* (starred review)

"With the skill of a virtuoso, Dee plays his character's shifting voice over its full emotional range—cunning, desperate, cynical, resigned and more. At barely more than 200 pages, *Sugar Street* is a novel that easily can be consumed in a single sitting. But that brevity is deceptive, because it's far from a simple book, and the feeling of unease it induces makes it an unsettling reading experience." —*Shelf Awareness*

"Compelling and thrilling . . . Dee's impressive versatility is on display once again in this scintillating and entertaining tale." —*Booklist*

"This propulsive and furious book is as fun to read as it is relentless and unsparing. Deranged and faltering America, Jonathan Dee has your number."
—Joshua Ferris, author of *The Dinner Party*

"A deft punch of a novel . . . Dee creates a true page-turner out of simple materials and the result is a troubling and stimulating look at real American life—at the fix that materialism plus the information state has got us into. It's also very funny."
—George Saunders, *New Statesman* (UK)

SUGAR STREET

Also by Jonathan Dee

The Locals
A Thousand Pardons
The Privileges
Palladio
St. Famous
The Liberty Campaign
The Lover of History

SUGAR STREET A Novel

Jonathan Dee

Grove Press
New York

Published simultaneously in Canada
Printed in the United States of America

First Grove Atlantic hardcover edition: September 2022
First Grove Atlantic paperback edition: September 2023

This book is set in 11 pt. Berling
by Alpha Design & Composition of Pittsfield, NH.

Library of Congress Cataloging-in-Publication data is available for this title.

ISBN 978-0-8021-6119-2
eISBN 978-0-8021-6001-0

Grove Press
an imprint of Grove Atlantic
154 West 14th Street
New York, NY 10011

Distributed by Publishers Group West

groveatlantic.com

23 24 25 26 27   10 9 8 7 6 5 4 3 2 1

THE AMERICAN INTERSTATE highway system. Wonder of the twentieth-century world. Smooth, wide, fast, inexhaustible; blank, amnesiac, full of libertarian possibility; burned onto the continent like the nuclear shadow of the frontier spirit, even if you happen to be traveling east instead of west, not much difference anymore. Route 66, Jack Kerouac, all that shit. But at some point I snapped out of it and remembered the truly salient, nonmythological fact about the interstate of today, which is that law-enforcement cameras are everywhere. You can't travel ten miles in any direction without your movements being logged, your license plate photographed, your face. Certainly once you're on the highway, there is no way to get off it again without all those things happening, without your whereabouts becoming data, instantly. Right. No more highways, then. I pulled my hat down over my eyes and got off at the next exit, drove around until I found a nonchain gas station, bought a 3 Musketeers and an old, folding paper map of the state. They still sell them. I remembered my E-ZPass, another data bomb, and threw that into a construction dumpster I passed a while later.

First days of summer. Sometimes, on the right or left, through the tight canopy of green, an unexpected glimpse of water. All the windows rolled down, even though the AC works fine. A sign welcoming me to this or that town: a couple of traffic lights, a kind of drawing together of buildings, then gone.

And then I'll be on some long stretch with nothing but scrub on either side and suddenly there'll be a house, out of nowhere, miles from any intersection, set back only maybe twenty feet from the road. Who lives there? Why? What's their job? Sometimes when I'm tired, I'll see one of these places that's so geographically estranged I think maybe I'll just pull into the driveway, knock on the door, and offer to buy it, for cash, on the spot. Be somebody's dream come true. But no, that's not the answer. I have a plan, and I'm sticking to it. I don't slow down.

Candy and coffee, candy and coffee. Under the passenger seat is an envelope full of money. Ill-gotten? I mean, I guess. One of those heavy, waxy, interoffice envelopes, the kind with the string you wind around two buttons to close it, so it can be reused. Ten by thirteen. It fits easily in any kind of suitcase, but it's a little bulky to carry around on its own. I try not to get too attached to it, but it's also hard to get too far away from it without experiencing some symptoms of panic. That's not the only reason I slept in the car the first two nights instead of at a motel, but it's one of them.

The chain gas stations—chains of any kind—are operated by and for remote multinationals, and the paradox is that the billion-dollar operations are always the ones with their eye on every penny: thus the security cameras. Citgo, Valero, QuikTrip, Sunoco, Getty, Hess, Circle K: bank on it, there are cameras there. Ones you see and ones you don't. And it's all a network, so your face on one of them is exactly the same as your face on all of them. Chain motels, similar principle. And there aren't a whole lot of independently owned roadside motels out there anymore, outside of horror movies anyway.

I'm old enough to remember when the paper maps were the only maps. You can't really look at them and drive at the same time; you have to pull over, memorize your next few steps, and then get back on the road again until you're no longer sure where you are. Mileages are an approximation, done, sometimes, with the tips of the thumb and index finger. It is nice not to have your phone startling you with instructions all the time. I backed over my phone in the driveway three days ago, and I miss it less and less. Sometimes I listen to the radio. Talk is best. Another way to measure distance or progress: I find an angry voice and I listen to it until I've driven far enough that I can't make out what it's saying anymore.

This diner where they had something on the menu called the Defibrillator: can you imagine? I wanted to order it but lacked the nerve. At the counter I stared at the hard back of the cook, who looked like someone trying to stay sober, trying to stave off trouble. Tattoos crept above the neckline of his T-shirt. Waitresses yelled at him loud enough to make me flinch, and he never gave an indication of hearing a word. He went at the filthy grill like an action painter. All these newly enviable lives.

Empty barns with their roofs collapsed, walls leaning, foliage growing out the windows. The first one looks artsy, but by the time you see your tenth one it just comes off as spite.

I estimated five days but it's going to be more like seven or eight, because I find I can't stay on the road as long as I thought I could. My eyes start to hurt. By now people are looking for me, though probably not in the old-fashioned, Butch Cassidy sense where I turn around and see stubborn figures on the horizon. They're hunting me with their ass glued to the chair. They'll find you that way, too, if you're not careful. So I'm careful.

The summer insects so loud, when you get out of the car to take a piss, it's hard to believe the engine could have drowned them out.

The money is mine now, though that won't stop other people from maintaining that at least some of it is theirs. If anything, their lives will be improved once the hole in it, where the money and I used to be, heals over. Still, people who were close to you—or who believed they were close to you— they're going to want to know why.

The difficult part, at night, is finding a place that's unpatrolled, a place where no one will call a cop because they saw a car parked where it shouldn't be. Anyplace you can pull off the road and not be seen is good. My back hurts, my knees hurt. I could use a shower. Once in a while I pass a place so Bates Motel–looking that I think surely I can risk it. Surely there's no surveillance in there. Surely if you just show the cash they won't ask you for any ID. I have no ID at this point, neither fake nor real. I cut up my driver's license right before I hit the road. Which means I have to stay at or below the speed limit at all times, signal every turn, come to a complete stop. I'm the most law-abiding driver in America.

The next town is like some weird hipster paradise, but at least there's a drugstore there that's not a chain. An artisanal pharmacy, the sign says. I buy some aspirin. The knee pain is getting harder to bear; it's more from the cramped sleeping than the driving. At least I think so. Worse this morning than last night. The guy behind the counter, who has a stiff beard and an apron like a fucking blacksmith, asks if I'm in town for the festival. You bet, I say.

Back in the car I get out the map and plot the day with my fingertips. You can't drive highway speeds on two-lane roads, obviously, not if your goal is to avoid any risk of getting pulled over, so it's taking me a while. I figure I can still go three hundred miles before dark, if the pain permits. But the pain doesn't permit.

I resort to some magical thinking. I tell myself that I won't go looking for an independently owned motel, but if I happen to pass one, that'll be like a sign, and I'll let myself check in there. A mattress. A shower. If they ask for a credit card or insist on ID, I'll make like I left my wallet in the car, then go back out to the lot and just gun it. A mattress. A shower. These ideas start to exert the kind of force that sleep exerts when you haven't had enough of it for a while.

The lady asked for payment in advance, and I asked if cash was okay. She said they took a credit card just as a deposit for incidentals. I said, What incidentals do you offer? I wasn't being sarcastic, but she took it that way. She said it was really a guarantee against damage to the room. I said I didn't have a credit card at the moment, but I was happy to leave with her as large a cash deposit as she thought was fair as long as she wrote me a receipt for it. She said, kind of pointedly, like calling my bluff, Five hundred dollars. I said, Sure, okay. Let me just go out to the car for a second. By now she probably had me pegged as a fugitive. But the real point of this story

is that after we both went through with it, after I'd gone outside and come back with the money and she started writing
out a receipt on a piece of blank paper she pulled out of the
printer, she asked me for my name, and just like that, I had
to decide what my name was going to be. I mean, I wasn't
committing to anything. It was just for that night. But still.
I wish I'd thought about it more.

There was a time when I might have lost my temper in an
interaction like that. And when I say "there was a time," I
mean like a week ago. Interesting what happens once you
start to feel vulnerable. I seem fainter, even to myself.

The grim palette of those cheaply paneled rooms. Suicide
Ochre. And the sheets and towels have a special texture:
worn but not soft. I started to get paranoid about the lady at
the desk (the owner of the place, surely, she seemed way too
nervously invested to be some employee) and even peeked
between the curtains a couple of times to see if she was anywhere near the car. When it was fully dark I went back out to
the lot, unlocked it, and pulled the envelope out from under
the passenger seat. I took it back in, went to the bathroom
(because no windows), spread one of those ancient, translu-
cent towels in the tub, and dumped out the money—just to
count it again. No reason.

$168,048.

That's a lot, though it doesn't really matter how much it is once you've accepted that there will never be any more of it, only less. Even if you only buy two Diet Cokes and a 3 Musketeers one day, at the end of that day, that much less is left. Like one's days on earth, in that respect: pure subtraction. I put the cash back in the envelope. No bill larger than a hundred. I went to sleep with it beside me under the dermabrasive sheet and woke up well before dawn, only to realize I would have to kill time until six or so anyway, when the motel office opened and I could get my deposit back. Right, the deposit! $168,548, then. Sweet.

While the sun rose, I watched some TV news in the room. No change.

I pulled back the curtain again, half expecting to see the lot filled with police cruisers, guys with hats and sunglasses bracing their gun arms on their open driver's-side doors. But no, just three other cars. I tried to remember if that was the same number of cars parked in the lot when I arrived, but I hadn't thought to notice. I'll have to become a more observant person going forward, more disciplined.

When the office opened, it wasn't the woman behind the desk but a man, who could only have been her husband. His expression suggested he'd been brought up to speed on me. Before I finished unfolding the receipt he was reaching beneath the counter for the five hundred dollars. Asked if I was checking out and even though I'd been looking forward to just lying with my knee fully extended on that lumpy bed with the shades drawn for an hour longer I said, Yes, thanks, everything was terrific. Gave him the key. He did not inquire about damages. Breakfast came from the vending machines on my side of the desk: peanut butter crackers and a Diet Pepsi. He watched me pull the knobs like these were going to be important details later.

Positive, as I drive away from there, that the wife wrote down my license number, either last night or this morning. One hundred percent. Probably the most exciting thing that's ever happened to her.

Well, it was time to ditch the car anyway. I mean, it's in my name. There's something called a VIN—vehicle identification number—that connects it to me; it's right there next to the steering wheel, but I didn't have the tools to pry it off, and from what little I learned about cars on the internet the VIN is sometimes stamped on the engine block as well, which is totally beyond me. Even apart from the risk of getting pulled over if my plate is now flagged, the longer I wait to get rid of the car, the nearer I'll be to it whenever it's found. Every mile I drive it now ultimately narrows the field of search.

Anxious all day, and by sunset I felt myself falling asleep at the wheel. I found a little turnaround for a plow, hidden from the road, and slept in the back seat. Nerves shot. The car itself feels radioactive now, glowing; in my dreams it pings like a submarine. A matter of time before someone finds it, and me in it. In the morning the knee pain greets me first thing.

Bought a new map. I estimate three more days.

And then on a county road in the middle of nowhere I pass a place with a wooden sign stuck in the ground: BODY WORK painted on it along with a phone number. Downward streaks on the sign, from its having been planted upright before the paint was dry. Maybe fifteen cars, parked haphazardly in the sun beside a barn. It looks like hurricane footage on the news. About a mile past it, I turn around and go back.

"You sell cars here?" I asked the guy. "Used cars?"

"Sometimes," he said warily.

"Or trade, I guess. You take cars in trade?"

He stared at me.

"Because I'm looking to trade this one," I said and smiled. No idea why I smiled. It didn't help my cause.

"For what?" he said.

"Just for something that runs. Something reliable."

"This one's unreliable?"

"No," I said. "This one runs fine."

"There's one thing I should say," I said. "I'm looking to do this off the books. No title, no registration."

"It's stolen?" he said. No change in his expression.

"It's not stolen. It's mine, legally."

"Got any papers?"

"No," I said. I'd burned those in my kitchen sink and washed the ashes down the drain. "I'm looking to exchange plates as well."

There was nothing else to say, or so I thought.

"You're a cop," he said.

"I'm not a cop. I swear."

"You look like a cop."

I'd never been told that before. My first thought was that he looked a lot more like a cop than I did. Like someone who worked out too hard. Behind the barn sat a trailer on concrete blocks, with curtains tight across the windows. One of the curtains was a Confederate flag.

"I'm not a cop. Look, if you're not comfortable, I understand. I'll keep looking."

He held up one hand. He turned around and walked into the trailer, emerged a few seconds later with a set of keys. He pointed to a gray hatchback that had one of its wheel wells rusted away but was still probably the most reputable-looking car of the bunch.

"Take that for a test drive," he said. "Up the road and back. If you think it's a fair trade, then it's yours. Feel free to look under the hood, too, if you want."

I know nothing about cars. I wouldn't recognize a problem under the hood unless maybe something was on fire in there. I was taking a huge risk—the envelope was still under the passenger seat—but I was a little afraid of him now, so I did as he said, and the hatchback ran smoothly. I parked in front of him—he hadn't budged—and got out with the engine still running, to take inventory of anything that might get me pulled over: headlights, brake lights, turn signals, license-plate display. Amazingly, everything worked.

"This'll do it," I said. "Thanks."

He nodded.

It took a few minutes to transfer everything from one car to the other. Bags, boxes, maps, trash, the money. And then, because I couldn't resist: "Can I ask you something? You could have squeezed me here if you wanted. I'm obviously not in a strong bargaining position. But you're giving me a pretty fair deal."

He looked done with me, with talking.

"How come?" I said.

"Because I never want to see you again," he said.

It's vanity to want some record of all this but I do. Probably for the best that there's no way for me to write anything down, much less type it or speak it into a phone or laptop or anything that runs on power, where copies of it are generated automatically and exist in perpetuity and can never be tracked down or eliminated. The Cloud! They should give some kind of knighthood to whoever came up with that bit of adspeak to gussy up the most terrifying development in human history. Then: I wandered lonely as a cloud. Now: iCloud.

Mysterious sudden unzoned hellscapes in which every fast-food restaurant on earth operates a franchise side by side. Not really urban, not really suburban. No one lives there. The road widens to six lanes to accommodate the traffic.

Finally, the first road sign with the name of my destination on it: 126 miles. I will miss the paper maps, though. They rebooted my relationship to space. Also, they were a kind of reading. At the last gas station—I mean the last one, in all likelihood, that I will ever stop at—I stuffed them all in the garbage can between the pumps.

$167,979.

Remember when hitchhikers were a thing? Haven't seen a single one.

A few fun facts about facial recognition technology and how effective it's gotten: In China, police officers are issued special eyeglasses capable of locating designated individuals in crowds. One man was pinpointed—and arrested—at a pop concert with sixty thousand fans in attendance. The software's algorithms run not just on what you look like but on what you used to look like. On what you will look like. People love to talk about how dangerously inaccurate it is, but what's scarier, really? When it makes a mistake or when it doesn't? Most countries—most states—have no laws governing its use by police or by anyone else. It's not like some advanced version of security-camera footage. That is, it's not something someone somewhere is reviewing to see what you did. It does that work all by itself, and it is looking at what you are doing right now. No consent to this type of surveillance is required, or even possible really. Just in case you think I'm being paranoid.

Made it.

Up and down streets, mapless, reconnoitering. The place looks surprisingly like I pictured it: houses close together, sullenly so, like people wedged on to a rush hour bus trying to ignore how intimately they're being touched. Strip malls, dollar stores, drive-through banks. Drive-through everything. School parking lots, empty this time of year. Road crews filling potholes, the stink of hot macadam, a wheelbarrow, two or three guys in filthy jeans leaning on shovels, crossing their hard arms.

Where to sleep the first night? The first few nights? Days Inn, Super 8, Courtyard by Marriott: nope, nope, nope. I saw a couple of big public parking lots, but you didn't have to try hard to spot the cameras mounted high up on the light stanchions: they don't even hide them. Little blue lights to show you where they are. So I left the city again, drove ten miles back the way I'd come, and parked on an unlit road. Feeling foolish but determined not to be careless now. I'll go back in the morning, early, and start looking for a place to live.

I've made a lot of mistakes. It's hard to draw breath in this world—to feed yourself, to work, to move from place to place—without doing damage of some kind. Environmental damage, human damage. It's hard to lighten your footprint, much less eliminate it. There's one sure way to eliminate your footprint, of course, but I was and am too much of a coward for that. Also too curious. Not optimistic: curious. If the candle of this world goes out for good, I kind of want to see it.

Newspaper classifieds are no use—if you're going to pay for a classified ad, you're likely going to want things from a tenant like credit checks and references. And the internet is obviously out of the question. So I'm driving around with my eyes open. Looking for poor neighborhoods, though not so poor that people would be too suspicious of the sight of me. Two-story places. Quiet streets, neglected streets, places run-down enough that no one meets your eye. Plenty of those here. I just need a sign.

Grove Street, Belleview Street, Elm Street, Grand Avenue. Names that evoke nothing, correspond to nothing, there only because a street has to have a name.

I didn't research this place as thoroughly as I could have, because that would have involved the internet, and even though I eventually put a drill through my motherboard, everything you do on the internet leaves a trail. Your first instinct might be that the best place to disappear would be the country, the woods. But no, it had to be a city, I figured: navigable by foot or mass transit, big enough to be anonymous in. Nothing too cosmopolitan, though, not someplace anyone of my acquaintance would go for vacation or for some conference or convention. I've never so much as passed through; I know no one here; I know no one who's ever even been here. Nothing to connect me to it: not the tiniest filament of logic or intuition to lead anyone who knew me to suspect that this is where I might have gone to ground.

I've done some harm. I've hurt people. And I've done it while priding myself on being kind, unselfish, a good person, which only makes it worse, because it suggests how little self-awareness I have, how unreal my will is, how pointless my intent. I left it all worse than I found it. I've committed some crimes.

ROOM FOR RENT—a handwritten sign on a piece of notebook paper. A phone number. Having no phone, I knock on the door. A woman answers, and she's younger than I expected. I take a step back, deferentially, and ask if the room is still available. Behind her, nothing but an artificial, shades-down darkness. She looks me over. "Sorry, no," she says and shuts the door. I walk back down the steps to the sidewalk. Across the street, two boys stare at me, not challengingly, but as frankly as if I don't even see them, as if I can't. I think today is a Tuesday, but anyway, it's about eleven o'clock in the morning.

Yards with grass so high it wilts. Corner stores with windows blacked out by lottery signs. An abandoned house with scorch marks still visible on the frames of the upstairs windows.

Two more nights driving back out of town just to sleep in the car. The only thing I can say with confidence at this point is that this isn't some trial, some experiment. There's no going back. I made sure of that. Only forward. This is it, this is my life now, to the end.

I just need to find a room, even if it's not permanent; I need to be behind walls, where my face is not exposed. Rolling around the residential streets in the hatchback, which is almost certainly stolen: how else would it have wound up in that guy's yard in the first place? Nothing connects me to the car, though, once I'm not in it. Possessions are chains, traps. This seems like a religious or monastic idea but it turns out to apply to the outlaw life too.

Sugar Street, it's called. Can't be too many cities with a Sugar Street, and this one is a million miles removed from anything to do with the growing or processing or packaging of sugar, so who knows. Somebody's fantasy. Anyway, driving up and down in some of the more featureless parts of town—trying not to travel the same block twice, to avoid attracting notice— I come across Sugar Street, and I get a good feeling, and sure enough, there's a house with a laminated cardboard sign in its cracked porch window that says ROOM FOR RENT INQUIRE WITHIN. Inquire within! Fancy!

I park right in front of the house—so that I can leave the money in the car but still have an eye on it—and by the time I'm halfway up the walk the owner has opened the door, stepped through it, and closed it behind her, with an aggressive look on her face. Strange, smiling men exiting cars: what good news could they bring?

She is quite a presence, instantly bigger than the modest physical space she occupies. Somewhere, anywhere between thirty and forty-five. Ink-black hair in a precarious bun, tank top and shorts, tattoos everywhere. Lots of words in the tattoos, in illegible cursive. Too much time in the sun. And the most peculiar shape: skinny legs, skinny arms, and a super-stout torso, breasts, stomach, everything, like she's been put together out of mismatched parts, some kind of chop shop of physiques. I mean, the parts probably weren't always mismatched. It's a drinker's body, was my first thought. She didn't seem drunk just then, though.

"Help you?" she said.

I said I'd seen the sign and wanted to ask about renting the room.

Her eyebrows went up. "No shit," she said, half a question. She didn't make a move to let me in. "That your car?" she said. I said I was borrowing it from somebody while I looked around for a place to live.

"Why don't you live with Somebody, then?" she said.

That bridge, I said, summoning up a little wince, is burned.

She nodded, went back inside, and shut the door. I stood there for a few seconds on the front step—a rectangle of plywood on cinder blocks, one of which was sinking into the ground—feeling watched, trying not to turn around. Sweat flattening my hair. Then the door inched open again, and she emerged with a ring of keys in her hand.

"Come on," she said. "Separate entrance."

That was a plus. The room was around the back and up a flight of external stairs. I hung back a bit, to avoid my face coming uncomfortably level with the back of her too-tight shorts. There was nobody else outside, on the sidewalks or the street, and every window I saw was covered. The fourth key she tried opened the door, and she walked in ahead of me, as if she wanted to make sure the place was empty.

But there was no question it was empty and had been for some time. The smell told you that. "Gotta leave these windows shut with no screens on them," she said and then struggled to open one window, but it wouldn't budge. I flipped a light switch to no effect. But in the sunlight I could see everything there was to see.

It was grim. One long rectangular room, narrow, with windows in the front and back. Dropped ceiling with water stains everywhere. Linoleum on the floor of the kitchen area, except for two missing squares in the corner. A rusty-drained sink and an unplugged fridge and electric stove with the coils missing on two of its burners. A moldy-looking bathroom off the kitchen. No bed. No furniture.

"There's a public middle school right down Sugar and around the corner," she said, which seemed like an odd selling point.

"How much are you asking?" I said.

She stared at me. I could see her deciding whether to give me the real price or one at which I might take offense, so she could see what would happen then, how desperate I really was. Every thought she was having, you could see it on her face: she cut a pretty formidable figure but in the guile department she had less going on than she probably imagined.

"Are you a sex offender?" she said.

"What? No."

"Because you seem kind of like a sex offender," she said. "That's why I mentioned the school. I could probably get into trouble for renting to you if, you know ..."

I shrugged and shook my head.

"Well, it's one seventy a month," she said. "Utilities not included. Payable in cash on the first, in advance. Plus one month's security deposit."

Security deposit! That struck me as pretty funny under the circumstances, but I kept treating her seriously. "I'll go two hundred if you include the utilities," I said, because of course I couldn't set up any accounts like that in my own name. I also thought that negotiating might make me less suspicious in her eyes, and it did seem to do that. But there was still something she didn't credit about me.

"I can't have any trouble here," she said. She didn't say why not. It was like her imagination was running away with her: whatever had brought me there, it had to be bad if she couldn't guess it.

"No trouble," I said. "I can give you the first six months up front if you like."

Her eyebrows rose again. "You can't park that car here," she said, trying to recover from seeming pleased. "No space for it."

"Like I said, it's not mine. After I move in, it'll be gone."

Fourteen hundred dollars cash was what was written on her face. Still, there was something more malevolent than greedy, I felt, in her desire to take me at my word. Not a sound from downstairs. She jingled the keys in her hand.

"What's your deal?" she said. "You do something? Somebody looking for you?"

I met her eyes. "No," I said, as convincingly as I could. "Just looking for a fresh start."

"Well, we'll give it a shot. I don't know what your deal is. But I'll tell you this," she said, laughing as if she'd put one over on me. "I was pretty much going to give it to you no matter what, because I put that sign up back in April and you're the first white one who's come around."

And I'll admit I laughed too, a little, just to make the contract.

IMAGINE YOUR BIOGRAPHER. Let's say it's a she. She sits at your kitchen table and she's polite and respectful and full of enthusiasm for the task at hand, which is to gather up everything there is to know about you, the record of your life. There are some things in your past that you would just as soon she didn't know about, and you're relieved when she seems not to know those things, at least not yet. After a few hours, she can see you're tired and so she thanks you warmly and goes out into the world to interview everyone who's ever been close to you, patiently, perhaps for years, at which point, she says cheerfully, she will be back to follow up.

It's not just the suspense over whether she'll learn what there is to be learned. It's knowing that the time, however long or short, between now and the day of her return is all the time you have to alter the record.

I figured out where the Goodwill is and bought some furniture. Nothing too big to fit in the car, nothing too big for me to carry up those back stairs by myself. So that meant a futon, which I unrolled on the floor against the interior wall. I'm getting used to it; at a minimum, it beats sleeping in the car. And it does have the upside, when I'm lying on it, of preventing me from being visible through the windows.

A card table with collapsible legs, two metal folding chairs, a deep, canvas camp chair that also folds and is surprisingly comfortable. The futon and a comforter and some sheets. Haven't figured out where I'll wash them. A pillow. A trash can. Silverware and a couple of plates and a coffeemaker and a pot. They have everything at the Goodwill, and except for the loading bay in back, they do not have cameras.

She watches me through her blinds. If I wave, she waves right back, so she isn't hiding, exactly. I paid her six months in advance, as promised, utilities included, so there's rarely any occasion to speak to her.

She dresses the same every day: shorts, two or three layered tank tops, hair piled up on her head. Hard looking. Her clothes are all tight. Maybe she likes being provocative, or maybe they're clothes she bought years ago and they don't fit the same now. Her name is Autumn, or so she told me. I'm in no position to be skeptical of anyone's name.

$165,406. The envelope, for now, is underneath the futon.

After much painful banging with the flat of my hand, the windows open, and the smell exits like a reluctant spirit. The front window faces roughly east, so I had to buy some kind of curtain if I didn't want to wake up with the dawn every day. Also a curtain rod, a screwdriver, and some screws. The next time I saw Autumn, she gave me a little sarcastic lip purse and said, "Look who's handy."

I thought about a TV, while I still had the car to transport it, but for a TV to work, you need an antenna, and I don't know. An antenna in my home? Signals go two ways, whether they tell you so or not. I compromised on a radio. I went to Goodwill every day until one appeared: a very pleasing old clock radio, as it turned out, the kind with an actual dial. That's the beauty of Goodwill; they're not just restocking the shelves with the same items, reordering as things sell out. It's passive, even random up to a point. Everything depends on the circumstances of the people who show up at the loading bay door with stuff they need to get rid of, intimate circumstances you'll never know.

No phone book, no computer, so I spent an entire day driving around the edges of town looking for some kind of auto-salvage yard, someplace raggedy enough that I could hand them the keys to the hatchback and walk away. I never found one. Or I found two, but they looked too reputable, and I couldn't figure out what to say to the men I saw there, how to explain the kind of transaction I was looking for without arousing their suspicion. So here's what I did: I made sure every trace of me was out of the car—wrappers, napkins, everything—and drove until I found a service road off the highway, near some kind of spooky runoff pond. No houses there, no structures of any sort. I pulled into the scrub, and when I was convinced I didn't hear anything except distant traffic and insects, I wiped the car down with my shirt for prints inside and out, I threw the keys into the pond, and I walked away. The only part of this plan that felt less than genius was that I was now several miles from home. Also, I didn't quite know how to get back there, except in a rough, follow-the-sun kind of way. I didn't want to ask anybody where Sugar Street was. I didn't want to ask anybody anything. So it took me almost four hours, though to be fair I did stop three times just to rest and get something to drink. It was close to ten p.m. when I found the house; I felt like crying. She pulled aside the curtain and watched me limp up the driveway toward the back stairs, the flickering light of a TV framing her head.

Now everything that can identify me is corporeal, unsheddable: blood, DNA, face, fingerprints, voice, retina, whatever. Not much I can do about any of that. They say that when you undergo a bone marrow transplant, if you survive it your blood type and DNA actually change. Fascinating, though obviously not something one could consider, you can't just walk into a hospital and ask for a transfusion of someone else's stem cells a la carte. In any event, I've done what I set out to do: I've gone quiet. I emit no signal. I cannot be triangulated. I'm Tom Joad. I'm nobody—who are you?

Even so, it's not easy to let your guard down. The fear of being seen is ingrained, reflexive. I hear cars slow down on the street outside and step back from the window. I avert my face when strangers pass me walking the other way. I try to calm myself, to remind myself that no one knows me here, that this is a big country. But most people have no idea how thorough state surveillance is today, how complete and invasive and perfectly unscrupulous. The moment you feel like you can relax—like you've left your pursuers nothing, you're a cold trail, you've won—that's when you're most likely to slip up, according to the laws of irony anyway.

Peak summer now. Humid and still. Not much better at night. The radio informs me that we are poised to break a record. At least I don't have to talk to anyone about the weather, because I don't talk to anyone about anything at all. There's a decent cross breeze in my room when the front and rear windows are open, but my futon is too low to the ground to feel it, so sometimes I will get up in the middle of the night and sit in the camp chair in the dark to cool off.

I could never really cook. A life of fast-food takeout would do me just fine, in theory, but every inch of those places is camera-covered. The counters, the drive-through, I wouldn't doubt the restrooms too. So I have to find diners, roadhouses, people running restaurants out of their homes, their back-yards. There's more of those than you would think.

For instance, just six blocks off Sugar Street, it turns out, is the best Korean restaurant in the history of the world. It doesn't even have a sign outside, apart from a laminated square of cardboard in the front window that just says OPEN. It looks like—in fact, it certainly must be—someone's house. The kitchen is just a kitchen. Beyond it there are four tables, never more than one of them occupied, and yet the menu is eight pages long. Six blocks is a ruinously long way to carry any kind of noodle dish involving broth, so once in a while I'll take a risk and eat in. Sometimes a woman will come out of the kitchen, nod to me politely, and then seat herself at the table next to mine to roll out dumplings.

It's not a hairshirt situation—the Goodwill, the thrift-store clothes. I'm not martyring myself. I miss nice things. Plush furniture, art on the walls . . . But if you want to live beneath notice, this is how it has to be: no accounts, no subscriptions, transactions only of a certain immediate type, in certain unpatrolled venues. Nothing escapes the world's attention like a poor person. Of course I am not a poor person. I know that, every one of my deprivations is a choice. Still, I am living the life of a poor person, and, increasingly, I look like one.

She says she's the owner of the house, which would be good news for me but also strikes me as unlikely. She doesn't have a car; there's a bus line I've seen on Grand Avenue, and that must take her wherever it is she goes. I've seen her wearing scrubs. Once in a great while, when I'm lying in the dark but not sleeping, I hear low voices: through the floorboards, through the vents. Could be the TV.

The soul of the radio is dark as pitch. It used to be the mainstream, bland corporate realism, but then technology moved forward and what's left behind is mostly just rage getting shot into space. Something ugly is eventually released when you keep talking and talking with no idea who's listening to you. Like some Cro-Magnon version of the internet. Anyway, there is a local AM station, which is useful for me, but when it turns to nationally syndicated talk around drive time I find I can't tune in for very long without starting to feel angry myself.

The gradual process of replacing all my clothes. Bought a short-sleeve, button-down shirt today at a place called Thrifty Shopper, took it home, took off the shirt I wore to the store, stuffed it in the trash, and put the new one on.

I should feel happy. Triumphant, even. I set out to do the impossible thing in this bugged panopticon of a world—step outside it, remove myself from it, cancel every claim on me, not by killing myself but by conceiving and then stepping into a second, empty life—and I did it. I am noncomplicit. There were a lot of cords to cut, and I cut them all. Opting out was not a course others would have granted me, so I had to make it happen. It required not only careful planning and discipline but also a revolutionary hardening of my spirit. Still, I guess there is a sort of mourning period, even for yourself, even for little deaths that you alone imagined and then personally brought about.

$164,745. I think it's important to note that I didn't ruin anybody. I just want that on the record, even though, of course, there must be no record. I could have, but I didn't. I didn't clean anybody out. I took what I needed, though that need was challenging to calculate. They'll be all right. They might not see things that way, but if I concerned myself with how others see things, I'd be right back where I was.

There's a bodega a block and a half from the house that sells beer, but they have a big camera right over the door, in a mesh cage. There's a safer one about twice as far away. I only buy one six at a time, even when I could carry two. Keeps me from overdoing it. Tempting, some nights, to polish off the six in one go just to put myself to sleep, but what lies down that road? Nothing good.

The initial plan was to spend some time covering my new home city by foot, getting acclimated, forming a kind of aerial layout of it in my head. Once the fear of being seen had worn off a little, that is. But it is so hot. Ninety-two yesterday, the radio says. Even with a hat, after twenty or thirty minutes on the sidewalks the sun dizzies me. There's also the knee issue, though the heat actually helps with that, most days.

So: more time than I imagined in this room. I won't compare it to a jail cell, it's much, much bigger than a jail cell, and anyway I've always flattered myself that I'm the kind of person who would do okay in jail, not socially, maybe, but mentally. It wouldn't break me. But that doesn't mean I want to go.

Outside my front window, growing on the sloped strip of grass between the sidewalk at the end of Autumn's yard and the street, is a remarkable tree. I don't know what kind of tree. I have gone my whole life without learning how to tell one tree from another, one plant, one star from another. What's remarkable about it is that it has a huge network of long, thick limbs but only about four or five feet of trunk. It looks like someone hammered it too hard into the ground.

The airport must be pretty nearby. When the wind's a certain way, flight paths take planes more or less right over my roof. The last time I was on an airplane—which, come to think of it, was the last time I will ever be on an airplane—there was some kind of commotion during boarding, some delay.

31

Nothing violent, no raised voices, but suddenly there was a gate agent on the plane, and the captain, joining a knot of people in that sadistically narrow aisle. I was sitting near the back. A flight attendant breaks off from the group and heads toward me with a smile on her face and also blushing a little bit I think, though it's hard to tell; they wear so much makeup. I look at her as she gets closer, my heart starting to pound—am I in trouble? What did I do? What's with the smile?—but she just sails right past me and stops a couple of rows behind.

"Sir?" I hear her say. "There is a gentleman in first class who would like to switch seats with you." I turn around and she's addressing a guy in military uniform. I noticed him when we were boarding, not so much because of the camo but because he looked about seventeen years old. He's staring at the attendant, not moving, polite but confused.

"To thank you for your service," she says, and I must have made some kind of sound, because the strangers sitting directly behind me both turn their gazes away from this exchange and regard me blankly, just for a half second, like synchronized, before turning back.

The kid sheepishly stands, grabs his carry-on, and makes his way up front. A minute or two later, some older dude wearing expensive clothes walks past me, takes the grunt's seat, and I swear to God, the people in the humiliating steerage class of this commercial airplane start *applauding* for this fascist, leaning over to shake his hand. What a selfless aristocrat! Thank you so much for giving this kid the thrill of experiencing Delta's first class, before you put a high-tech gun in his hand and send him to the other side of the world to kill some unwhite people he doesn't know for the protection of profits he won't share in!

I'm not a big "thank you for your service" guy, let's just put it that way. I wished someone else in first class would switch seats with me, so I could spend the flight grilling this dim teenager about what he was doing and why, what kind of sap he was to think that executing his government's murderous commands in exchange for a break on college tuition would make him into a man. Make him admired. Except it did, right? Everybody on that plane admired the hell out of him, and they admired the hell out of that robber baron who was sending him off to kill or be killed. It was just me. I was the one who didn't belong. And that made me a little sorry for myself. I hadn't yet learned to move toward the not belonging. Instead, all I had with which to try to dampen my anger was the thought that if that plane went down and I was taken out of this world, at least both of those death dealers would leave it with me.

I don't know what made me remember that story. Yes I do: the planes flying overhead. But when you're sitting in the same chair all day and part of the night, I guess the past is just going to seep in, that's all there is to it. Good luck trying to wall it out.

$164,522.

I went to the woods to live deliberately. Is that how it goes? I had room in the car for a box or two of books. But they felt like evidence. I left them where they were.

Eventually the weather breaks, and I can get out a little more. The bodega, one day, had a street map for sale on the counter by the register—just one—and I bought it and taped it to the back of my door. I don't carry it with me. I don't want to look like a tourist, especially in places where no tourist would ever go. I walk and explore and come back home and look at the map to see where I've been.

The main arteries here are not pedestrian friendly—the sidewalk stops and starts—and so I take mostly side streets, and I get lost quite a bit. Residential streets, where you don't want to linger. Downtown I'd be less conspicuous, but it's a long walk from where I am, and besides, there's a level of risk there. Cameras all over. I wear a hat at all times, and sunglasses. I've stopped shaving.

She must wonder why, if I have no job, I leave in the morning and come back at night. Maybe she thinks I am engaged in some great criminal enterprise. She stares at me, unsmiling. She doesn't really have to interact with me until the end of the year, when the rent is due again.

The number of churches seems disproportionate. I can walk a ten-block rectangle and come across five of them. It's an immigrant city—I know that much about it—which may explain some of that dark Catholic grandeur. But then there's the Al-Zahra Mosque and something called the Casa de Restauración that clearly used to be a showroom of some kind, until they covered up the windows and slapped a sign over the door and bam, a house of God.

I don't get it. I don't admire it at all, never have. First off, organized religion—all of it—is mostly just codified misogyny. That's a fact. But whatever I may think of it, it's still out here doing its retrograde work. Every time I walk past one of the older ones, doors propped open in the heat, no matter the hour, I see a handful of people in there.

Total severance from yesterday is the goal, but that's difficult when your memory insists on replaying the same few scenes over and over, looking for loose ends, ways you might have revealed yourself without even knowing it. One bit of recent history I can't make my brain stop looping: I'm haunted by the stupid answer I gave Autumn when she asked me what my "deal" was. "Just looking for a fresh start." Jesus! Things shady people say. I'll probably get that question again at some point, if not from her then from someone else. I need to be ready with a story that sounds plausible without getting incriminatingly close to the truth:

My deal? I had a child—a daughter—and the child died. She was sick for a long time. I would love to be able to say she didn't suffer. How she suffered is something I can't discuss. Her mother and I were already divorced when she got sick, which is one of many things I will never forgive myself for. We came back together for her but I get why my wife can't stand the sight of me now, the sound of my voice. I, too, can't bear to see anyone I used to know, anyplace that featured in my former life. I can't bear it that all of that didn't die along with her. So I left in order to become a stranger, to be surrounded by people and places with absolutely no sympathy, no affinity for me. It numbs the pain of opening my eyes every morning.

(Not terrible. A little over the top, but it wouldn't surprise me if Autumn has a maudlin side.)

Or maybe: My deal is that I care about the future of this planet—not of human beings per se, human beings can and probably should go fuck themselves right into extinction for all I care, but of this planet. I worked for a while in the nonprofit world, me and my nifty law degree, and what I learned was something I should have already known, which is that the idea of reforming murderous governments by appealing to said governments to reform themselves is worse than useless. So I went outside the law. Let's just not get any more concrete about it than that, for your sake and for mine. I went outside the law and that is where I remain, and there are powerful people who would label me a terrorist because labeling someone a terrorist grants you license to do anything you want to make them go away. I have chosen instead to make myself go away. For now.

Mid-August. I try to get out when I can stand it. The sidewalks on my block, the rickety porches, open or enclosed, stay empty almost all the time, at least when the sun is up. At night it's darker than a city block should be. I'd thought at first that the streetlights just weren't working, but then I saw that each of them was cracked wide open. How? Probably by shooting at them? I wish I'd been here when that happened; it must have been a party.

No place to go, no place to be. No interactions, no relationships. That's when you can feel time passing, doing its work on you. I mean actually feel it. The day tingles like stepping out of a bath. I can feel time on my skin.

What connects you to other people? Selfish instincts, mostly. That and the internet. I don't miss the internet as much as I thought I might. It lasted a short while, that dopamine withdrawal they talk about, but then it went away. Not surprising, really, since I lived for years without the internet before somebody thought to invent it. All that instant connection to the world, to friends and strangers, to "the news," it feels like the human condition when you're in it, but when you're outside it you see that all along it was just a product, something sold to you so relentlessly every minute of every day that you forgot it was transactional at all. Then at some point there was something called the internet of things, a phrase I never really understood, but anyway I am now all about the internet of the senses, which can't be monetized or hacked, limited bandwidth maybe but the privacy controls are outstanding.

And then, on my perambulations, a discovery: a public library. A terrible one, but still. It's not even that far off Sugar Street— maybe a fifteen-minute walk—despite how long it took me to happen upon it. They have daily newspapers, which is huge. They have a music room, but it has an Out of Order sign on it that looks old. They have leather chairs, and the chairs are half-full of men about my age, dressed about like I am, groomed about like I am, staving off vagrancy.

Went back again today. A thick brick square, probably considered ugly at one time but aged into nostalgic dignity. Named after someone I've never heard of. High ceilings, a round dome above the checkout desk, open stacks, lots of light. And air conditioning! I thought I'd learned to live without it, but when it took me by surprise, I felt a purely physical relief almost to the point of tears.

Books have clearly lost the battle for floor and shelf space over time. There are magazines and rows and rows of CDs and VCR tapes. And long tables holding a total of eight computer terminals. Free access to the internet. In an instant I am that close to my old self and thus to an answer to the question of whether and how I am still being looked for. I could find out. I don't remember all of my old passwords anymore, but I remember most of them.

But when I walk casually by the checkout desk, I see the laminated sign spelling out the rules for use of the computers, and Rule 1 is that you must show some form of ID. So that takes care of that. My only glimpses of that realm will be whatever sites other library patrons happen to be looking at when I pass behind them. I'm pleased to see that the monitor cameras have all been covered with masking tape; at least someone thought of that.

When I walk outside again, I look for a cornerstone and find one: 1915.

It's appealing, comfortable, quiet, a place to go. And then I return home one afternoon from my third or fourth outing to this library and at the bottom of the exterior stairs, sweat-soaked, I see that my door is open. I consider running but then I hear a voice, Autumn's voice. I get up there and she is not alone. There is some dude in chinos and a work shirt with a logo on it. She looks at me with a little smirk. He does not look at me at all.

"Inspection," she says. "For energy efficiency or whatever. It's annual. They do it for free, but then they try to pressure you into buying storm windows or some shit. A total scam."

This probably explains the stoic, let's-get-this-done look on the face of the inspector.

"You weren't home," Autumn says, "and this was when the appointment was scheduled, so . . ."

I wait for what seems like half an hour while the inspector gets to his knees to shine a light into my heat register and then struggles to his feet again. They leave, and I stand with my fists clenched until I hear them clear the last of the exterior stairs; then I lock the door and do a full-on belly flop to get my hands under the futon. The envelope is still there. I dump it out on the bed and count it. Still there.

But the lesson is that she feels free to enter the room when I am not home. And so, even though it is obviously not a viable solution long-term, I don't leave the room for the next four days.

I try to come up with a backstory that might scare her off a little, though some finesse is required since I am not a scary person:

My deal is that I am in witness protection. I can't tell you why, Autumn, because it's much better that you don't know. Better that, if someone should come around here asking, you'll be able to tell them in all sincerity that you don't know a single thing about me. That way they'll leave you alone.

On the last Monday of August, noises out my front window early in the morning, and when I got up and peered out: children. Two or three, then more, then a stream, all moving in the same direction. Like an arroyo dampening and then flowing after a storm. All different ages, some in groups of two or three or six, some alone. They were aimed, I realized, at the school: school was back in session. I'd forgotten all about it. But now here they were. Some trudged straight ahead without stopping; others procrastinated, hitting each other, chasing each other. They reached out and touched that low-slung tree at the end of the yard as they passed it, like they were happy to see it again. Maybe a quarter or a third of them wore headphones or earbuds, squeezing every second of music out of the day, right up until they entered the school and were forced to remove them, or so I imagined: I'd walked past the empty school building many times but whatever the rules were inside of it was a mystery to me. Anyway, kids with their ears covered or filled so that they couldn't hear the collective noise they made, but that noise was all I could hear for half an hour in the morning and then, in the afternoon, for a longer time, because there was less of a rush about getting home. That limbo, the in-between, that's what was theirs, and they occupied it as long as they could, unselfconsciously, performing only for each other, no sense whatsoever, even in the middle of a public street, that anyone else might be watching.

CALLING A LOCKSMITH and swapping out the cylinder on my door would surely count as a violation of my lease, if I had a lease to violate. Still, what I want is peace of mind, not a confrontation. At a dust-rimmed, fantastically overstocked little hardware store called Feeney's, I buy a hand drill and a deadbolt kit with a key. When I see Autumn go out, I go to work and have the whole thing installed before she gets back. It's pretty flimsy. Two or three good shoulder blows would probably break it right off. But it's only Autumn that I'm worried about, and even if she possesses the physical strength, which is doubtful, it's tough to imagine her going that far.

So now I can go out again. Back at work trying to internalize the grid of this place, to develop a more instinctive sense of direction. It's small enough for that. Sometimes a bus passes me, though I have no feel yet for routes or destinations. But all that will come. I have all the time in the world here.

Finally made my way, cautiously, downtown. Newer, taller buildings, more aspirational restaurants, an air of prosperity, or maybe just belief in prosperity. A plaza with a skating rink in the middle of it, not operational now of course but repurposed as a sort of concrete playground with fountains for kids to run through. That was nice, the plaza, but on the whole I didn't enjoy it down there. I passed a window that advertised "Wealth Management." Never have I wanted to break a window more in my life.

Picked up an oscillating fan at Goodwill that works well, if a little noisily. I watch the children walk right to left every morning, then left to right in the afternoon. How can I put this? In the aggregate—or on average—they are conspicuously less white than the neighborhood itself. Not that I'd call the neighborhood an especially white one, it isn't at all, but still. And languages reach me through the window, totally unfamiliar languages, not like Spanish, which I don't speak either but can at least recognize when I hear it. Igbo? Tamil? I have no idea. I'm only guessing.

So they, like me, are not from around here. Once or twice I have caught myself hurrying back home in the afternoon to be in my chair in time to see them pass.

On the flagstone path between the sidewalk and the library entrance there is a kind of community bulletin board, a neatly curated array of flyers and announcements protected by locked plexiglass. Of course, people just tape things directly on the plexiglass and obscure whatever's beneath, which gives the whole thing a pleasantly anarchic, vox populi vibe. Today

I saw a sign for a rally downtown to protest a police-involved shooting. I've heard about it on the radio—the shooting, that is. The victim was sleeping in a parked car. Anyway, at the bottom of the sign, in large letters, was this legend:

SILENCE = VIOLENCE

I'll never vote again, never sign my name to a petition or expose my face to cameras at a rally. Politically, I guess you could say that I'm a progressive. I firmly believe that everything in and about human society is progressing toward its end.

"What is that?" Autumn says, laughing. "Is that supposed to be a beard?"

We've run into each other at the trash bin. Not every man is equally hirsute. It's not considered a marker of virility anymore, not like it used to be. Nowadays men are more obsessed with getting rid of their hair.

"Please, enough," she says. "You're killing me. You look like you used to have a beard and the chemo is making it fall out."

It seemed like a pretty sensible move, for a man trying to alter his appearance. But it doesn't work for everyone. Apparently.

The girls walk together, the boys walk together. The groups interact, but they are still distinct. Coed groups are rare and usually appear to be composed of siblings or maybe cousins. On the way home they will sometimes stop and sit, in pairs, on that short-trunked tree—inside it, almost, like a gazebo. They extend their arms to take selfies in there.

There is a girl, in full hijab, who catches my eye because she walks with a younger sister or cousin and steps in front of her whenever she hears a male voice. I don't think she even knows she's doing it. Unlike the others, almost all of whom carry backpacks so impossibly stuffed they look cantilevered, she carries her books in front of her, holding them across her chest with her folded arms. Where is she from? She excels in school. She's at the top of her class. I know it. I can tell just by watching her. The others mock her and try to get under her skin, probably. Imitate her cruelly whenever graded tests are passed back. She doesn't care. I am a great supporter of hers. I don't know her name.

A cartoonishly broad array of body types at that age.

You have to make your world smaller. That's the idea, I think. Our connections are too many, too thin. Not enough difference between the real and the unreal, and as a consequence we lose our sense of how to treat other people.

It's a poor city, but of course there are rich people in it. Rich neighborhoods, rich enclaves. I walk through them as well—uneasily, because I don't look like I belong there, or maybe I only flatter myself that I no longer look like I belong there, maybe the part of me that looks like that is the part of me I can never take off. Anyway, there's a neighborhood called Stone Farms (I know this because it is carefully bordered by signs saying WELCOME TO HISTORIC STONE FARMS), which seems to have become a kind of privilege ghetto, if that makes any sense. People who have declined to join the exodus to the suburbs, those little white hamlets I will never see. People who "love old houses." They imagine they are doing something positive, something liberally noble, by not ceding the city's "historic" neighborhoods to the hordes who would not value architecture or preservation or landscaping. It's a class nostalgia that runs so deep they aren't even aware of it, or they mistake it for nostalgia for something else entirely, like Arts and Crafts. The streets are curved rather than straight.

Another reason I speed walk through these particular streets: cameras. Over every front door, every back door, every garage. Not law-enforcement cameras, true, so less inherently threatening. Still, I don't want my presence recorded on them.

I will say this for myself: my footprint is pretty tiny now, like a baby's footprint. Maybe there's an environmental case to be made for what I've done, the path I've chosen. You must make your life smaller. Scale it down. Resources are scarce: it's arguable that the most generous thing you can do for the other people in your life is to stop depending on them.

To the editor: I can't help noticing how many of these anti-police protests take place on weekday afternoons. It says to me two things: 1) they don't have jobs, and 2) they don't like waking up before noon. Maybe the second thing has something to do with the first?

Every edition of the local paper gives two whole pages to letters like this, surely because it dawned on somebody over there that unsolicited correspondence from readers is the one type of editorial content that doesn't cost them anything. The paper itself is a disappointment; I guess I was clinging to some romantic idea about local papers delivering local news, but no, it's mostly wire-service human-interest crap and listicles. Husband and Wife Married 67 Years Die Minutes Apart.

The letters, though, are addictive. The boilerplate fears they express are not that remarkable—it's more the pride that's taken in them, the fact that they were shaped into the form of a letter at all, the faith in the idea that one's nastiest, least generous thoughts aren't fundamentally private but cry out to be shared, maybe in order to make others feel less alone. Some of them read like they were dashed off in a fit of reactionary anger, but others, you can tell, were worked on with some care. Signed, too, let's not forget.

I remember reading that somewhere around 2045, white people will be the minority in the USA. God, what a glorious day that will be. I mean, in theory: in practice, it's going to be war. I only hope to be around to see it. If white people had a tombstone, it would read, "They Stopped At Nothing."

What a cesspool this world is. Democracy, capitalism, liberalism: all in the lurid end-stages of their own failure, yet we won't even try to imagine anything different, any other principle around which life might be organized: we would sooner choke each other to death, which is basically what we're doing.

The children flow back and forth every weekday like some tidal river, but no child ever joins the flow from this block. They come from wherever they come from, south to north in the morning, north to south in the afternoon, like passengers on a train that runs by here but doesn't stop.

One of them is named Haji, or Hajji or Hodgie for all I know. He is the tallest, though he seems young for his height, and he is always either well ahead or well behind the group, so they must constantly yell to him, which is how I know his name. He smiles a lot, but it is a vandalous smile, a smile of apology-in-advance for whatever transgression he knows he is helplessly about to commit.

Of course I can't individuate them all in my memory, but I try to, because it becomes a kind of game or challenge to see which of them attend school all five days in a given week and which don't. Some of them pop out from the crowd, of course, and become memorable, become personalities. There's one boy—smaller than the others but strong, wiry— who, every day, when he passes the streetlight stanchion nearest the corner, grabs it and hoists himself outward until he is perfectly horizontal, parallel to the ground, like a flag in the wind, arms extended. He then drops to his feet and looks around to see who has watched him do this, who is impressed. They never give him the satisfaction of looking at him. They just keep walking, and, after a few seconds, he resumes walking too. Every day.

$163,929.

The Goodwill: all women, usually with children in tow. Different faces, but all on the same palette somehow; I don't mean racially or ethnically but emotionally. Embarrassment, anger, excessive joviality, numb blankness: all related, all from the same root. Some of them look like they are trying not to be seen, and some of them look like they are hoping you'll say something to them just so they can go off. They stare at me, because, lest I forget, I'm the novelty in there.

The bodega: women in the daylight hours, men at night. The cash register is behind heavy plastic—clear plastic once, now mysteriously smudged and scratched. There is too little floor space to loiter in, but some of the men do anyway, and consequently it is one of the few places where I sometimes see people smiling. Midpoint faces: thirties, forties, fifties.

Squinty, sun-beaten. There is a small deli counter that has one single orange sitting on a plate behind glass. I can't bring myself to buy and eat it because I have little confidence it would ever be replaced.

The library: well, it's like a river or a brook, with a steady flow in and out (all female) and then the estuary or tidal pool of those who hang out there as long as permitted (all male). Black faces, white faces. Shabby clothes but not smelly or offensive. Everyone is friendly but also a tad nervous, aware that this place is like a ledge and if you slip off of it, what awaits is the world of less respectable group settings, of shelters and Medicaid homes. Apart from the kids whose mothers whisk them past us on their way to the Children's Room—and from the mothers, too, I guess—mine is one of the younger faces there.

To the editor: So-called children who commit violent crimes (DA MET BY PROTESTERS OUTSIDE LANGHORNE TRIAL, Sept. 21) should be tried and convicted as adults. Kids grow up a lot faster these days. As for what they grow up into, that is the fault of their parents. If we keep excusing everybody because of their "difficult" upbringing, then the streets will continue to be full of roving packs of thieves and violent gang members with no sense of morality. Why should law-abiding people pay the price for certain segments of society's refusal to take responsibility for their actions?

Friday afternoon and the children are extra vivacious on their way home. They yell at each other: the boys in a laughing manner, the girls not so much. One of the boys stands intimidatingly close to one of the girls, as they often do, just a kind of test of their own power. The hijab girl, the one without the backpack, comes to the rescue of the other girl, who is near tears. She directs a torrent of invective at the boy, who does nothing until Haji gives him a look or perhaps says something too softly for me to hear; then the boy hands back a hair clip or barrette of some sort. The scrum breaks up and flows on toward home, out of my line of vision. But there is something in the grass bordering the sidewalk. A green notebook. I've seen it clutched to the hijab girl's chest many times before. Pretty much every day, in fact. Other children straggle past, and they glance down at the notebook as they pass, but they don't stop to pick it up, they leave it there. Half an hour after the street is empty, I am still at the window.

I feel there might be a way to intervene, to put this right, without risk to myself and without copping to the fact that I watch the children carefully enough to have any idea whom that notebook belongs to.

I could put up a sign: LOST NOTEBOOK. But I can't give a phone number, because I don't have one, and to direct the owner to knock on my door would expose my existence on the block and would seem objectively creepy besides, like a trap.

I could stand out there Monday morning, holding the notebook itself, waiting for its owner to recognize it. But that exposes me to every single one of them, not just the notebook's owner.

She probably needs it to do homework. I watch and wait, thinking she might retrace her steps, might get special permission from her mother to go out even though it is near dark. Perhaps her mother will insist one of her brothers accompany her. Does she have brothers? I haven't the faintest, I am making up her family in my head.

The greenness of the notebook itself fades with the light, making it invisible. Monday is three days away. The wrong kind of person could pick it up; it might have personal information inside.

The radio says rain.

I wait until the sun is almost down, until the humid air is murky and gray. As noiselessly as I can, I open my door and walk down the exterior stairs; the inside of each step, nearest the house, is quietest. Autumn's lights are off. I walk down the driveway to the sidewalk, looking around me in every direction, and I kneel down and pick up the green notebook. It's thin, like it's had pages torn out of it. I don't know if I'll be able to resist the temptation to look inside it but right now it's too dark to read anyway. Holding it down at my side, I walk quietly back toward the stairs. The rain hasn't started, but the air is full of it. I'm still not sure what I should do next, but my hand was forced, I had to preserve my options, I couldn't just leave it out there to get ruined.

A soft click or swish, like an animal noise, but I turn and it's the sound and sight of a match being lit. Autumn is sitting on her doorsill, feet resting on the plywood sheet that rests on the concrete blocks, lighting a cigarette, watching me for maximum effect before shaking the match out.

"The fuck are you doing?" she says.

"I saw this lying on the sidewalk," I say. "It probably belongs to one of those kids who walk back and forth here to school. Just figured I'd grab it before it got rained on."

She's a little drunk, bright-eyed. She looks skeptical, but exaggeratedly so; she's not suspicious, I realize, so much as pleased—pleased to have caught me doing something of which I might feel ashamed. "Yeah," she says, "that seems totally normal."

"Well, what are you doing out here then?" I say.

"Just having a cig," she says. "I love this kind of weather. Not rain, but the release, if you know what I mean. Look at that sky, it looks like a fucking bruise. Here," she says provokingly, scooting over the few inches that she can, "why don't you join me?"

There is really not room for both of us to sit on the doorsill. I could sit on the plywood below her; maybe that's what she means? "I don't smoke," I say, as if it's a compromising or emasculating thing to admit, as if I've said I don't know how to drive.

"A drink, then." From beside her leg she lifts up what looks like a giant 7-Eleven go-cup and tilts it back and forth temptingly at me. "Come on. We only have a few minutes anyway. Or are you in too big of a hurry to get upstairs and beat off to that kid's diary?"

I would trade half the money in that envelope upstairs to feel one raindrop right now. Instead, I lower myself to the plywood more or less at her feet, the notebook in my lap.

"I had this older boyfriend when I was about seventeen," she said. "He had a thing about thunder, the sound of thunder. Like a kink. No matter where we were, if we heard it, he'd give me this look, and we'd just go find someplace."

She hands me the go-cup; there is no second one. It smells sweet and vile.

"Southern Comfort and Diet Coke," she says. "You're not an alcoholic or anything? I should have asked first. Because you look sort of like an alcoholic. I mean, a sober one."

If candy could go bad: that's what it tastes like.

"How have we not done this before?" she says. "Why are you so shy?"

She laughs, meaning that second bit as a joke.

"You know what the Levenson test is?" she says. "Ever heard of it?"

"No," I say.

"They've given it to me a couple of times. I'd like to give it to you. I'd be curious to know your score. It's very accurate, supposedly." Autumn takes a long last draw on the cigarette and then stubs it out and tosses it into her yard. "So what's it been, like three months now?" she says. "And you've been, what's the word, a model tenant. I mean, the first few weeks I was convinced you were making a bomb up there or some shit."

"Nope," I said. "Nothing like that."

"You'd be a pretty unlikely terrorist, though. A sleeper. That'd be a deep fucking sleep!"

She laughs, and I laugh too.

"Although I did google that name you gave me," she says. "And it's obviously fake. But that's cool. I'll get it out of you. And in the meantime, it's kind of like I have some dirt on you." She pantomimes a sort of evil eye and then laughs. My vision blurs. She is wearing a tank top and scrub pants, though it is almost October. "So what do you expect to find in there?"

The notebook she means. "Nothing. I mean, I'm not going to read it. One of those kids is probably looking for it. Maybe I'll put up a sign or something."

"Sure. That's not at all creepy."

"They just . . . who are those kids? What kind of school is that? They seem like they're not from around here."

"What was your first clue?" she says. Gently, she takes the go-cup back from me for a turn with it. "They're refugees. There's city housing, Section 8 housing, Catholic Charities housing, I don't know what all, down by Jefferson Square, and that's where they all live. This city fucking loooves to take in refugees. God knows why. Government money, probably."

She smells a little bit. She's repulsive, but sort of admirably repulsive: like a queen might allow herself to be repulsive, because what are you going to say to her? She's the queen.

"Refugees from where?" I ask.

She shrugs. "The fuck do I care?" she says. "Listen, wherever they come from, whatever fucking hardship they've had to overcome or whatever, they're animals, basically, just like most kids only worse. They carve shit in my tree, they throw their garbage in my yard, they steal whatever isn't nailed down. I can see from your face that you're one of those types gets a boner thinking about the plight of the poor refugee but let me tell you something. Whatever these kids have gone through, it's made them worse not better. Not their fault but so what? They're nightmares."

Frantically, silently rehearsing, even as I'm nodding along and smiling weakly and looking up at the threatening sky:

My deal is that there is somebody out there who wants to kill me. Let's just say it's not a scenario I could expect the cops to help with or even believe, probably. Telling you my real name would have put both of us in a bad position.

"What about you, though?" I say: a strategy that really should have occurred to me ten minutes earlier. Maybe it's the Southern Comfort. I gesture at her scrubs. "You a nurse?"

She blows out smoke. "Like a nurse," she says. "Like two steps below a nurse, I would say. I catch shifts where I can. This city is a shit place to live but it's got good hospitals."

"How did you wind up here? Were you born around here?"

She blows out more smoke. "Born around here," she says. "Lived here my whole life. Well, that's not true, I left for a while and came back."

I say nothing. The air is like a wet shirt.

"I inherited this house," she says. "I'd never laid eyes on it before. My mother died—I didn't know, I hadn't laid eyes on her in a long time either—and the court tracked me down and said because she died without a will, it was mine now. How she got ownership of it in the first place, I don't know. Well, yes I do. She was getting her claws into men all the time. Anyway, it was kind of a godsend, the first helpful thing she ever did for me, because at the time I had, as they say in court, no fixed abode."

We hear, before we feel, fat drops of rain on the pavement; and in seconds, the whole sky has opened up. "And there it is," Autumn says happily. She turns to me, smiling. "You better run for it," she says.

On the futon, on the floor, staring at the ceiling, where the rain pounds like it might break right through. Then it stops and I can hear the blood in my ears again. I don't know what time it is.

Googling me? There is nothing to google. And yet the terror I felt took me outside my body even as she was talking. I still can't calm down.

Here's an answer neither Autumn nor anyone I used to know would likely understand: my deal came down to privacy. I got to the point where I couldn't stand being exposed all the time—I mean, just in the routine way all of us are. It was getting to me, mentally, emotionally. I couldn't stand being seen as data: everything I did or said, everywhere I went, usable, profitable, predictive data. That invisible record, it accumulates, and you drag it around with you even though you can't see or feel it. I couldn't stand the idea that every little choice I'd made, however thoughtless or dumb, was now part of my history.

B UT THE NEXT DAY, the fear has passed; in its place, a renewed self-admonition to look only forward, to think only forward. Faulkner was wrong: the past is so past it's not even funny.

Here's what I did. On Monday morning, I went out to the sidewalk just a few minutes before I knew they'd start streaming by and I put the notebook in the crook of the tree. Risky, because someone might get there before the girl and grab it just out of curiosity.

But then, just as I'd imagined, or predicted, or dreamed—as if she were a character I'd invented, acting according to dictates only she and I understood—she came out early. Her sister-or-cousin was with her, but the older girl was ten strides ahead. When she saw the notebook, she stopped dead and her shoulders slumped, with relief I assume. She waited for the younger girl to catch up with her, and then, as the two of them passed the tree with the little girl chattering away, she grabbed the notebook without breaking stride, added it to the stack her crossed arms held against her chest, and walked on out of sight.

I still don't know what was in there. I never looked. But it did have her name on the cover: Abiha. Grade 8. Her last name, too, and her address, but those I will not repeat, though I remember them.

And I'll admit, it made me feel pretty good. I mean, I have to laugh at myself, at what an outsize satisfaction this gave me, like doing something nice for a stranger was an idea that no one had ever come up with before me. It's just that my interactions with people, over the years of my life, had grown more and more complex, secondhand, remote, filtered. Which made it easier to do harm. After L'Affaire de Notebook, I sat around for two days feeling a silly sort of rush, wondering when another opportunity to perform a small act of anonymous kindness might come along so I could score again. The fact that the beneficiary of my kindness was a person of color was part of the rush, then it wasn't, then it was again. I returned to the act in fantasy and embellished it, imagining versions where she accidentally saw me or where she opened the notebook and found, miraculously, some money inside.

I don't anticipate ever getting another job. It'd have to be off the books, obviously, day work, and who would hire someone who looks like me for that kind of labor? But even beyond that, I'm not one of those people who Needs to Work. The whole culture of employment: what does it serve, really? It serves the cause of maintaining the world as it is. You're like a particle of blood circulating through the way things are, and the way things are is pretty fucking toxic, terrible, destructive, nasty, vicious, brutal, and corrosive. In exchange for some money? No. Not anymore. Pass.

Which means of course that the money I do have is a finite resource. But I knew that. From the beginning I was budgeting for myself only a certain number of years—I won't say how many—but my new life has a strange and surprising feature, which is that I am spending almost nothing. So if money equals time, for me, then at my current cost of living I have a lot more time left than I imagined. It is not inconceivable now that my envelope full of cash will outlast me, as long as nothing about my present situation changes. And that flicker of possibility makes me even stingier, more selfishly protective of my little status quo.

So a kind of security descends and blurs the borders of the days. Boredom may become an issue. Not boredom. An unease, a restiveness. A feeling that all of this, the astronomical unlikelihood of my plan's success, must have been *for* something.

You must make your life smaller, scale it down: maybe that was the answer all along. It's a mindset, but I can see now that it's also, more plainly, about technology: bereft of technology, you are thrown back on your senses, and your senses, you might say, only have so much storage. I can't believe some of the things I used to know a lot about—celebrities, politics, culture—things that had nothing to do with me at all. Only disconnect, you might say, if you were still the kind of person who said shit like that.

And it happens naturally. That desire to cover the city on foot in order to contain it in my head: it's gone now, and my movements have scaled down even further, reduced to the web of my daily needs. The laundromat. The camera-less bodega that sells beer and the newspaper. Even better: my movements now accord with the weather. If it's raining out, I stay in; if it's hot, I wait until later when it's cooler. This simple equilibrium with the world brings me a sort of submissive peace. I know I am only discovering something that until very recently in human history did not require discovering at all.

I mean, my phone used to tell me, "You have a new memory." Jesus!

There are eight houses on the block, four on each side of the street. Autumn's is on the west side, two lots in from the south side, so slightly closer to Fourth Avenue than to Willow. It is painted white. Seven of the eight houses are painted white; the eighth, on the northwest corner (thus invisible from my window), is a weathered green. All of the houses are two sto-ries. I have tried to determine whether the other houses are all single-family dwellings, unlike this one, but I can't really see the comings and goings at most of them without standing in the street or on the sidewalk in a way that might be noticed. Parking regulations appear not to be enforced; I know this because a red Dodge Challenger has been parked in the same spot on the block since the day I moved in.

There's a park not far from Sugar Street, with a cracked, weed-split tennis court, and a soccer field, and a drained swimming pool. Hiking trails, over and around some of the small hills that characterize the terrain around here. I followed one that terminated at the base of a statue: two men standing in old-fashioned dress, studying a proclamation or manuscript of some kind. The statue itself overlooks the city, but the figures' eyes are down. I got up close to the base to read the names, and the names were Goethe and Schiller.

Goethe and Schiller! It felt like the end of *Planet of the Apes*. Probably some local citizens' group, some German-American Society, raised the money for it a hundred, a hundred and fifty years ago. Now they were nearly lost in the trees. In another decade or two they would be able to confer in peace. Dead white men, refusing to look up.

I do have some thoughts about the world. I think they're valid, worth hearing. Of course, who doesn't think that? But the difference—or maybe the opportunity—is this: I'm nobody. I don't mean "a nobody," in the sense of being unimportant or powerless (though I am those things too); I mean I am literally nobody, I don't exist. There is no particular agenda anyone could ascribe to me, nothing anyone could use to dismiss my thoughts as biased or agenda-driven instead of engaging with them. This is the world we live in now: no messages, only messengers, and you can always discredit the messenger. But no one knows who I am, what I am, where I am, so I couldn't be judged, except on the quality of my observations . . . Worth thinking about. A manifesto, of sorts, although one would probably need to use a different word, as that one has been hijacked, hasn't it, by its association with killing.

The paper lists "tag sales," and sometimes I go. A good, secure, unsurveilled way to pick up little gadgets I didn't even know I wanted, like a box grater. Priced to move at a dollar. What induces people to put price tags on their accumulated stuff and invite strangers into the house to pick through it? Recent death, probably, or sudden indigence, or maybe just a powerful impulse of vandalism directed at one's own choices. Every knickknack a haunting, a symbol of the options one might still have if one hadn't given in. The people doing the selling never seem in a good mood.

Her behavior has been odd, since that evening sitting on her doorsill. Jittery. Sees me and turns away. It's also possible that I'm trying too hard with her. It's difficult not to wonder what she'll do with the fact, now out in the open, that my name is an alias. Perhaps there'll come a moment when she wants something from me and will consider that she has the leverage to get it. For now, though, I'm sure she's enjoying the power dynamic between us, one-sided even by landlord/ tenant standards.

She did ask me if I ever gave that girl her notebook back. I won't repeat what she asked me after that.

I went to the library for the first time in a while. I had it in mind to look up this Levenson test that Autumn mentioned that night. I asked the sad, lank-haired librarian if they had a card catalog. Naturally they don't; they moved all that to computers years ago. Okay, I said, so I'd probably have to sign up for one of the terminals—

No, she said, that's a separate thing. The catalog terminal is right here. Look, it's connected to all the other libraries in the county, so if we don't have a particular volume but another branch does, we have an interlibrary loan system so we can get it for you—

Connected, I said.

Yes.

Well, no thank you, that's okay. Thank you very much for your help though. I appreciate it.

She gave me a look of grave mistrust. I retreated to the leather-chair area, and there was another man sitting there—a man I recognized from previous visits—a gray-haired Black man who wears polo shirts, some short-sleeved and some long, always buttoned all the way up to his neck. He smiled and beckoned to me with his finger.

"I have a card," he whispered, "so if you ever looking to check something out, let me know. I can do it for you if you want."

"Thanks," I said. "That's kind of you."

I'm getting a little sloppy in terms of precautions, losing some of my habitual paranoia, for better or for worse. If something like that had happened even a month or six weeks ago—someone remembering me well enough to identify me, to address me—I never would have set foot in that library again.

The first snow! "Unseasonable" would be an understatement. It came overnight, to give one the impression of having slept for a month. Not even high enough to cover the tops of the grass blades in the unmown yards.

Back to the Goodwill, then, in search of a decent winter coat, and it is mobbed, like a Black Friday sale. Advance planning is one of the casualties of being poor. Sufficient unto the day, or however that goes. Anyway, I leave with nothing.

"Take therefore no thought for the morrow; for the morrow shall take thought for the things of itself. Sufficient unto the day is the evil thereof." The library does have a Bible.

And by the time I get home that afternoon, the snow is gone.

Children go missing, from my perspective that is. They're there and then they're not, and usually if they're gone more than a couple of days, they don't return.

Abiha, of course, is my special one now. She has never been sick a day; or, if she is sick, she powers through it. She has the kind of impatient manner that comes from great intelligence; every time someone says something to her you can see in her face that she already understands and they are taking too long.

Wake up in the morning feeling more hopeful somehow. Unencumbered, all potential. This experience is changing the way I see. I'll go so far as to say it has made me optimistic, even if the radio won't shut up about how winter is coming.

With no warning from downstairs, there is a brief irregular banging and then the heat comes on, accompanied by a smell that mercifully spends itself after the first two hours or so.

The whole manifesto idea, on further reflection, seems vain. Words are vain. It should be about *doing*: silently, anonymously, and on the smallest scale possible. No third-party involvement, no observer bias. That's the aspiration. And there is an opportunity here, a unique opportunity of my own creation, if I can just figure out what it is.

The paper runs a story about the local refugee center. There's no news about it, it's just a profile, an evergreen they probably update every year or two. There is more than one such center in the city, but this one, I recognize, is in the neighborhood. Families come from Burma, it says, from Sri Lanka, from Eritrea, from Syria, from Somalia. The city has a long history of welcoming refugees, one that goes all the way back to the Underground Railroad. The story is a kind of feel-good piece about the city's generous heart; in two paragraphs near the end, though, comes a reluctant-seeming mention of recent events: funding to the centers cut, enrollment at the center's free English classes down because of fear of immigration authorities. Fear, that is, of making those authorities' job too easy by gathering together in one place for an hour or two. Also, there have been demonstrations, public demonstrations, against the centers themselves. People with signs, people with flags. Police having to ensure the refugees safe passage in and out of the building. There's a photo of one such police-escorted passage, and there are children in the photo, but I don't recognize any of their faces.

Five p.m., the clouds reddening from beneath, and there is a knock on my door. There's only one person it could be, but it's not her.

"Good evening," Haji says. He is smiling broadly, as he has probably already learned he must do around white strangers. "I hope I am not disturbing your dinner."

I can feel the flush rising from my neck to my face and am helpless to stop it. The sound of his voice—which I have heard before but never below a yell—is unsettling. His smile wavers.

"No, not at all," I finally say. What can he possibly be doing here? He has come to ask me for something. But for what?

He has a speech prepared. "I am an eighth grader at the Wysocki Middle School. We are raising money for a class trip to the state capitol by selling candy." Only now do I notice that he has a sort of plastic briefcase dangling from his hand. He opens it. "The candy itself has been donated by a local business, so every dollar you pay goes straight to the school for the purpose of the trip. Would you like to help us out?"

Tell me about yourself, I want to say. But this conversation, now that it is a conversation, feels perilous in so many ways. I nod, but he does not see me; now that his pitch is finished, he is finally looking past me into the room itself, and his expression is one of confusion.

"I don't get many visitors," I say.

"The lady downstairs," he says. "She told me to come up here."

"I'll take twenty dollars' worth," I say, and his face lights up. "Will you wait here a second?" In my head, I hear Autumn laughing. I close the door on him, not quite all the way, and I get down on my stomach to fish the envelope out from under the futon. Twenty dollars, he informs me when I return, gets me twenty candy bars. I pick out an assortment. I want to let him be on his way—I can see he is fidgeting—but I know that once I make my selection, our time together is over.

"What's your name?" I say instead, and he tells me. So now it's okay that I know it.

That night I sit in the camp chair, all the lights out, and eat two Mounds bars and a Kit Kat. Haji knows which is my window now. My sense of that window as a one-way mirror is gone. Pretty canny of old Autumn, when you think about it, which I do.

With the low temperatures, as with the high, comes a diminished motivation to go out. More time in my room. The heat, which used to come on and go off capriciously, is now steady and generous and has a narcoleptic effect.

Fire engines wake me in the middle of the night, and, unable to go back to sleep, I have the new experience of watching the sun rise while eating my last three candy bars. Frost has etched the corners of my window.

Twenty dollars. I could have given him two hundred or two thousand—pretty much the same to me. Sent all those kids to the fucking state capitol. But that would have made our interaction remarkable: a story to tell others, a window to point up to. The safest course, as ever, is not to attract notice.

December begins, and while my rent is paid through the month, I don't see any upside to waiting. I want to stay on impeccable terms. Once it's late enough in the day that there's no risk of waking her, I take twelve hundred more dollars out of the envelope under the futon, walk downstairs, and knock on her door. No answer.

No answer the next day, nor the day after. No sight or sound through the front window of her coming and going.

Maybe she knew she would be gone for a while and set the thermostat for my benefit.

I T'S 7:50 A.M., and no foot traffic on the sidewalk beneath my window, and at first I think maybe I've mistaken Sunday for Monday but then I realize: the school's winter break must have begun. Christmas is imminent, though I know this mostly from the radio.

So I turn it off. Nothing from downstairs, nothing from outside, nothing through the airwaves: it feels like armies of silence are gathering.

The next day, a patient, insistent knock on the door downstairs: Autumn's door, the front door. I can just see the top of a man's head; I have a better look at his van. I can see that he's holding a clipboard. When did a clipboard ever bode well? After three rounds of knocking—each the same, no increase in urgency—he looks around him and then starts to circle the house. For a moment he is out of sight and then his footsteps are audible on the back stairs.

He is certainly not a cop. He is wearing a tie, for one thing. A little lapel badge identifies him as an employee of the gas and electric company. He confirms this verbally.

"Is Autumn here?" he asks, almost sweetly.

The living arrangements are explained to him.

"Oh. Well, then, legally it's not your responsibility—just want to make that clear—but since it affects you, you may want to tell her when you see her that she is now three months in arrears on her bill, and so I'm here to serve her formal notice that her service will be cut off in ten days if payment isn't made."

He is a young guy—thirty at most—and, given the prickly job he has, I would expect him to be a little warier of people, less cheerful. Perhaps he is some kind of sociopath.

"There are city assistance programs she can avail herself of if she chooses. I'll slide these brochures under her door."

Avail herself. He is giving a speech. What sort of person could be this divorced, spiritually, from the nature of the work that he does? Almost every sort of person, is the answer. He is still talking. He has a script to get to the end of. It is amusing to imagine the change that would come over his face were he suddenly pushed backward down the stairs.

"Should the shutoff take place, the sheriff will accompany a technician from—"

The sheriff? Not clear why law enforcement would need to be involved.

"There are a lot of laws governing things like turning people's power off," the man says. "The sheriff is present to act as a witness that all of those laws are observed. Plus also, there is sometimes a confrontational aspect to, uh, to the act itself."

How much is the account in arrears?

"How much?" He flips through the printouts on his accursed clipboard. "Four hundred and forty-one dollars," he announces, "and sixty-one cents."

He waits, as requested, while the door is fully closed. A minute later I open it and press the money into his hand.

"Okay," he says, surprised but also happy. This will make him look good, to come back to the office with something to show for his efforts at collection. Tough, task oriented, not unmanned by compassion. "I can, I probably have the change, just to make it exact—"

His left hand is in his pocket, his clipboard temporarily held between his knees, as the door closes on him again.

$162,730.

She can't have sold the place. I would have seen buyers coming around, inspectors. It's the holiday season, when people sometimes have extended visits with their families. So that could be it. But her mother is dead, and Autumn got the house, which does not suggest the involvement of siblings.

I am probably overreacting. But here's the thing: with Autumn gone, I am squatting here. I have no lease, I have no identification. They could take me in just for finding me inside the house. It doesn't seem like too much of a reach to think that something bad may have happened to her, and if that's the case, I'm in an even worse position.

I have stopped turning my lights on at all. I am rationing cans of soup to myself; there is plenty more soup at the bodega, but I don't want to go to the bodega if I can possibly help it. I don't want to be seen leaving my room or entering it. The snow, when it falls, falls overnight and blankets everything. By day the ground records and freezes every footstep.

On New Year's Eve, I hear rare noises on the block, even through my closed window: music, thumping, shouting—party noises. All of a sudden they go from muffled to loud. There are young men in the street. And then the sound of gunfire. Five shots in a row, evenly spaced out. I am already lying on the floor, but I writhe closer to the window, underneath it, for protection. A sixth shot, followed by laughter. Celebratory gunfire, midnight, Happy New Year gunfire. The door shuts and the music muffles again.

Guns are yet another fundamental subject about which the life I've led has taught me nothing. I've never owned one, never held one, never fired one. Am I a little curious? Sure. I think everyone is. I'll bet it's very satisfying. Shooting in the air, though, seems an odd impulse to me. All risk, no reward. If you're going to do it, wouldn't the satisfaction be in aiming at something?

The walls of my room are blank, except for the street map taped to the back of the door. No new marks on it for quite some time now. Winter in these parts is about stoicism, endurance.

Huge, empty birds' nests, exposed now in the tops of the leafless trees.

First Monday after New Year's, school is back in session. I hear the crunch of footsteps on the snow. I don't risk looking out the window. If I can see them, they can see me, right? It's so cold that the whole procession takes only about half as long as usual anyway. Much quieter too.

I keep the radio on at such low volume that I almost have to press my ear against it to hear.

What if the guy with the clipboard wasn't who he said he was? What if he was some grifter who'd found a genius way to scare strangers into handing him cash? Lying on my side, facing the wall, I touch the register, and it's still warm.

Second Monday of the new year. The problem with shrinking your life down to a handful of pieces is that when one of those pieces is taken away, the effect is disproportionate. Knowing that one's thoughts or perceptions are irrational does not make one safe from them. It's the quiet, the isolation, the fear, the winter, the light bouncing off the snow. I am having dumb ideas. I think that if I lived downstairs, in rooms with actual furniture, I might be able to pull off posing as this house's owner if anyone came around. This starts to seem to me like a legitimate plan. I want to go downstairs and check for unlocked windows. The only thing that stops me is the likelihood of being seen.

I am supine on my futon, wide awake, eyes adjusted to the dark, when lights begin playing on my ceiling, filtered by the curtains. Red, blue, red: police car lights. I turn off the radio and wriggle over to the window like a figure in some movie about urban warfare, like a holed-up bank robber. There's a single police car parked at the end of the driveway, a single police officer—I can just see the top of his hat—knocking on Autumn's door. The surge of fear I feel almost causes me to pass out. Carefully, I slide back down so that my head is below the level of the sill.

After a minute, receding footsteps, and a few seconds later—the longest seconds of my life—I hear his engine rev and see the lights on my ceiling move and elongate and finally dissolve. I have to assume he didn't imagine anyone might be up here. I start breathing again, a little dizzy from having stopped. I look critically around my room, which contains nothing incriminating apart from myself, and the money.

Fear is humiliating, and humiliation, in its aftermath, breeds anger. Yes, I am technically a fugitive, still. I've done things for which I could be arrested, and there are almost surely open warrants with my name on them. So what? What difference does it make to a cop or to anyone else if I am here—an angry man in a lonely room—instead of some other place?

Whose interest is it in to put me back where I supposedly belong? Some would call it cowardly, pulling the old Irish exit on your own identity, on everyone and everything you knew. Well, I gave up a lot, materially speaking, in order to live by a principle. Call me a coward, then, call me whatever you want. I can't hear you.

THE NEXT MORNING, Saturday, half-awake, I hear noises from the baseboard heat register beside my head. Tapping, creaking; no voices. I put my ear to the metal. There is somebody down there.

Carefully, I stand and walk to the window. Footsteps in the snow, from the sidewalk to the front door of the house. They could be anyone's.

No one enters or leaves through the front door all morning, then all afternoon. It has to be her, I'm thinking by the time the shadow of the house itself has reached the sidewalk. Who else could it be? Still, the risk to myself is hard to discount. I'm Bertha Rochester up here. Night falls, outside my room and inside it, and the sounds from downstairs cease.

Noon. Slowly, quietly, I lift up my futon and take twelve hundred dollars out of the envelope. Downstairs, I knock gently on the front door and then take two steps backward into the snow.

She looks terrible. Her body thinner, her face fatter. She's wearing leggings and a bulky old sweater. The cold air swirls around us as we stand on opposite sides of her threshold. On her wrist is a paper bracelet.

"Not now, okay?" she says. "Later."

"I have the rent for you," I say.

"What? Oh Jesus," she says. "Come in."

And just like that I am in her home, the door shut behind me. She takes a step backward. A silence ensues, and to break it I reach into my pocket and pull out the twelve hundred dollars. "The next six months," I say.

"Oh sweet Jesus," she says in a strange, emotional voice, and she takes it from me, not roughly but gently, as if it might crumble into dust. I can't get a good look at the bracelet, but it seems like it might not necessarily be a hospital bracelet; it could also be from a concert or a festival or a club. It's yellow.

Autumn looks up and seems surprised that I am still there. "Well, listen, thanks," she says and moves toward me—for a moment I think she is going to embrace me—but she is really just taking the shortest path possible, which is more or less through me, toward the door. The room we are in is a sort of foyer or maybe an enclosed porch; there are two cushioned chairs made of bamboo and a coat rack and a mirror. Through the open interior door is her kitchen. I don't want to leave. I want to ask her where she's been, why she put me in such danger, whether such a thing can or will happen again. What I say instead, to postpone my departure, is: "The cops were here."

It's the wrong thing to say. "So?" is her answer. "So the fuck what? Is that your business? Maybe you're a cop yourself. That would explain a fucking lot actually."

"I'm not a cop," I say, not for the first time. On the kitchen counter I can see a pile of mail and a big, two-liter soda bottle with the label peeled off.

"Listen," she says, "I have things to do, so maybe just get back to minding your own fucking business," and just like that I am outside in the snow again, staring at her door. Strangely relieved, though, or maybe reassured is the word. For a minute there she seemed like her old self.

Next morning is sunny, and the children passing by on their way to school are mostly free of hats and hoods. Their heads are like closed buds, like harbingers of spring. But Abiha is not there, nor is her companion.

In the winter a kind of gray, all-encompassing cloud cover comes down some days like a pot lid, diffusing the light. Nothing casts a shadow.

On the streetlight pole outside the bodega where I buy soup and beer, there is a handwritten sign saying, ABOLISH ICE. Underneath it, in a different hand: AND SNOW.

The local radio is suddenly dominated by one story: a house fire on the west side in which two people died, an adult and a child. There are fires all the time—particularly in the poorer sections of the city, where buildings aren't up to code and tenants are living off the books. (Situations like mine, in other words.) But there is a twist here, which is that the fire was set. The occupants were a Yemeni family, plus some other relatives or friends, many more, in total, than anyone knew were living there. One voice on the radio says it was the result of some kind of family dispute. Another says it was the landlord, who hadn't collected rent from the tenants in months and wanted the insurance on the property instead (though if a landlord—or anyone else—were to hire an experienced arsonist, that person would have done a less conspicuous job than this arsonist apparently did). But the real flashpoint is the suggestion that neighbors did it, white neighbors, that it was a hate crime. This is the theory with the most adherents, even though or perhaps because there is no direct evidence to support it.

The address of the destroyed house is not Abiha's address.

I take a walk to the site itself, nineteen blocks away. (I'm pleased to realize that I know the route there without having to consult the street map on the back of my door.) I intend only to stand across the street and look at whatever's there until it stops being "news" to me. But when I get there I am surprised to see four or five other people who have apparently come to do the exact same thing.

There is no house, only a pile of ash and charred timbers spilling out of a small concrete foundation like a dead volcano. A miniature bulldozer sits nearby. The fire didn't do all this; I saw in the paper that the city razed what was left of the structure because it was deemed so unstable as to be a danger to the houses on either side, both of which are abandoned it seems, with plywood nailed over the windows. There's no more smoke, but the smell of wet ash is still everywhere.

The house is probably too far away from Wysocki Middle School for the dead child to have been a student there. I don't know why that matters to me, but it does. But it shouldn't. A girl died in her bedroom in a fire. How is that any more real if it happens to touch your own experience in some thirdhand way? Ego is all that is.

I feel uneasy, and when I turn my head I see that all four of the others on the sidewalk—one a couple, the other two solo—are staring at me. It's true that I don't resemble them. I'm not sure what they want from me. After a few uncomfortable moments I settle on shaking my head sorrowfully. It is deliberate and fake, even though I do feel sorrow.

After a brief whispered discussion between the couple, one of them breaks off and walks toward me. She is small and white, much younger than me, with a sort of Frida Kahlo unibrow that makes her gaze seem accusatory. She hands me a piece of paper and walks away without a word. Something about her clandestine manner makes me not unfold it until I'm out of her sight, heading back home. It's nothing but a date, a time, and an address. Above that is the familiar all-caps insistence SILENCE = VIOLENCE, and below it is a kind of stylized logo, some kind of clip art off the internet, that just says: FIGHT.

Fight whom, though? Fight what? Fight misfortune and horror? Fight the fact that the poor will always suffer disproportionately, that there will always be hatred and selfishness and lack of compassion? That there will always *be* poor people? I've got news for you, Frida Kahlo, you might as well declare war against yourself, because all those things you hate? They're in you. This is what it means to be human: to survive is to act selfishly, to participate in oppression, to consume more than your share in order to save yourself, to commit crimes. You can say, "Oh no, not me, I'm different," but what good does that do anyone, even if in your case it turns out to be true? The idea that humanity can somehow triumph over what's most awful about itself is narcissism. We're the poison, we're the virus, we're the fire, and the only way to stop it is to let it run its course.

Anyway, I take a pass on this meeting, or whatever it is.

It's about ten degrees hotter in my room than it was a week or two ago. She must be cranking that thermostat. I'd say she was doing it just to make me uncomfortable, but I remember how she's looked the last couple of times I've seen her—like she's freezing—and I know she's not giving me a thought at all. I open the window maybe half an inch and hope that the bitter chill outside and the sauna inside will make for equilibrium somehow.

Last month, if you include the rent I prepaid, I spent four hundred and thirty dollars. I guess that's something to be proud of, that I have grown able to get by on so little. Anyway, I sit down and redo the math. It's difficult because it involves calculating how much longer I think I'm going to live. But even the most selfish estimate leaves me, in lieu of a serious lifestyle upgrade, with more than I'll require.

After dinner, too early to go to bed, two beers in, thinking, thinking, and I hear someone on the steps leading up to my door. It is not possible for anyone to sneak up on me when I'm at home. In my camp chair, facing the window and so with my back to the door, I stop breathing, on full alert. The knock, when it comes, is so soft that I know it must be someone other than Autumn. But it is her.

"I was thinking about something," she says. She's wearing one of those oversize, full-length down coats, despite which she is shivering. I invite her in, and she ignores me.

"I'm undercharging you to live here," she says. "I mean, it's obvious. You're paying me six months at a time, like it's nothing. And so you ambushed me with the cash in hand and I took it, but we really should have renegotiated. You're going to have to pay more."

Her eyes are red, her skin has broken out underneath a thick layer of makeup. She looks bloated, puffy, and it's not just the coat. She is trying to fire up her usual intimidating expression, but it wavers, and something else is flickering underneath it.

"I don't think so," I say. "No. You can't just come up here and extort money from me when you need it. A deal's a deal."

"Well, you gotta go then," she says.

"Cool," I say. "Give me back my twelve hundred dollars."

Of course it's gone. I want to know where, though. Something about her refusal to be grateful for it makes me feel entitled to know. I'm not averse to helping, in some way. And what does she imagine happened to her electric bill?

"I'm paid up through July first," I say. "You want to raise my rent at that point, you're entitled, just as I'm entitled to go somewhere else if the rent is too high. We don't have a lease, but we have an understanding . . . Listen, you look like you need to sit down. You won't come in?"

Without a word she turns and walks back down the stairs, her hand on the railing the whole way.

I want to have pity for her, I do, but what is pity really? It's invasive; it's vain and presumptuous. It's not what she wants. And she's certainly not offering me any pity in return. She put me at risk. Now she's in trouble, and she could have asked me for help but she tried to bully me out of it instead. It's all about domination to her.

I didn't have to advance her all that money. I did it because it's in my interest to keep her somewhat stable, yes, but that doesn't mean it wasn't generous as well. It had an element of generosity to it.

And who ever said we needed to understand each other anyway? You know who she is, what she's about, what she believes. I mean, you know who she voted for.

$160,809. I bought a lighter comforter.

TUESDAY. Abiha absent for the seventh day in a row. There are a hundred possible explanations, but I fear the worst. I should have helped her when I had the chance, instead of pulling that self-indulgent fairy godfather shit with the notebook. What if I'd just given her and her family a few thousand bucks? Who would they tell about it, who'd believe them?

I can't face moving again. But if Autumn degrades any further, it might come to that. I find myself scanning windows as I walk around the streets for ROOM TO LET signs. And I am out more than usual, because the weather's letting up and because it's so goddamn hot in my room.

On Friday afternoon, the sun out, the sewer grates in the street noisy with runoff, I go out and walk counterclockwise around the block, slowly, timing it so that I will meet the first of the children on their way home. This is a novelty, seeing them up close, not from above, and it is almost too much for me. Not one of them smiles, or, if they were smiling, they stop when they see me. One group of boys starts to flow past me—I have stopped walking, I am stock-still on the sidewalk—and before I can stop myself, I say, "Haji."

He halts as if he's been struck. He stares at me, flanked by two friends, and I smile weakly. He's wearing a brown ski hat with an absurd pompom on it. I don't know why I didn't notice this when he came to my door that one time, but he is already taller than me.

"What you want, white man?" he says, and his friends laugh.

"Sorry," I say. "You came to my door one time selling candy for a class trip, and I remembered your name." I point up to my door on the side of the house. He continues to look at me rather than at where I am pointing. When I have nothing else to say, he shrugs and starts past me again.

"You know Abiha?" I blurt out.

He stops. His friends are listening from a distance. One of them has his hair dyed blond and cut in an impossibly high fade. "Abiha?" Haji says incredulously. "Man, who—"

"I used to volunteer at Wysocki. I knew her from there. Anyway, I said I would help her out with something, and I haven't seen her lately. You have any idea what happened to her?"

Haji looks deeply skeptical, but even among his friends, even in a situation where I am the vulnerable one, he is reluctant to confront someone who looks like me. "She gone," he says.

"Gone?"

He does not repeat himself. All this was for nothing. I don't know what I thought was going to happen. The warm winter air is suffused with my nonsense. I nod unconvincingly and turn to go.

"What you helping her with?" he says.

I try belatedly to act stern, authoritative. "It's private," I say.

"It's private!" one of Haji's friends says, delighted.

"Don't you want to help us, though?" says the other one, the boy with the fade, and explodes in laughter. Haji smiles too. Other children have stopped to watch.

My humiliation complete, I walk up the driveway toward the stairs that lead to my room. Everyone sees where I am going. "Help me, too, white man!" they shout after me, laughing. "Help me!"

What is my role in this world? What is my place? What a white question, to assume or even to imagine that I must have one. I thought I was disappearing from the world, but I don't even know how to disappear, I don't know how to picture the world without me in it.

And I am still so full of anger toward those who would diminish or embarrass me. I have so much pride. In fact my sins are uncountable. The very idea of flight from myself, from my identity, is laughable. Everything about me reeks of luxury. I try to imagine explaining to those boys who I am, what I've done and why. They would consider me insane. I have to do something positive for them, even though right now, if I could, I would slap them senseless. Amazing how quickly, how reflexively, the fantasies of violence take hold. They're not even an inch beneath the surface. This is why every effort to change the world has failed, is doomed to fail, as long as people are involved. Because people are a nightmare. Any system predicated on the idea of innate human decency is a joke. We're proving that now, as we have been for centuries. That hatred, that bigotry, that superstition, that deep, deep longing for petty vengeance: I can't step outside of that. It's in me and always has been. What you want, white man?

But the truth is I don't think all that much anymore about who I used to be, how I got here. I have always been here.

The sun stays out, and garbage dams the storm drains. For no specific reason—to satisfy my curiosity—I walk to the address that I remember from Abiha's notebook. It's not a bad little house. Two stories, peeling green paint, slouching, its lines less than parallel to the ground. No lights are on, the windows are uncovered, and there's no activity inside. I stand across the street and lean against a parking sign.

A handful of people pass by on the sidewalk, on my side and across the street, and suddenly one of them, a young man, pulls out a key ring and bounces up the steps to Abiha's front door. He shuts it behind him. I wait a few minutes and then stroll over, knock on the door, take two steps back, and smile.

It's not enough: when he opens the door and sees me, he closes it most of the way and sets his face in a hard expression.

"Hi," I say and give him a fake name. "I work at Wysocki Middle School, in the records department, and I'm looking for Abiha? Does she still live here?"

"No," he says.

"But you know Abiha? You know who I'm talking about?"

"No," he says.

I can't tell if he's lying. It comes off like a lie even if it's the truth, so strong is the imperative not to say anything helpful or cooperative to anyone who looks like me. He's very handsome himself, with tightly curled hair and wide-set eyes, not very like Abiha but not so different either.

"I have something for her," I say. It's actually true. In my pocket is a thousand dollars. "I have something to give her. Or her parents, her family. Do you know where they are now?"

"No," he says. This would of course be the moment when, if I were to really seem plausible, I would pull out some kind of business card and try to leave it in his hand, or even a scrap of paper with my name and phone number on it. The fact that I don't do this no doubt cements in his mind the suspicion that I am a cop or with immigration or at the very least that I am not who I say I am.

There is a liquor store four blocks down Sugar and one over, fortified like a bank, with barred windows, a cashier behind bulletproof glass, and, of course, cameras. If I do what I need to do to try to be undetectable to those cameras—hat, sunglasses, scarf—I will look like I have come in to rob the place. This is one reason why I have learned, since arriving here, to stick to beer. But today I go in there in full protective regalia, find a bottle of Southern Comfort as fast as I can, and take it to the window. I push a twenty through the slot.

"You want to take them shades off?" the cashier says, not amiably.

"Just came from the eye doctor," I say.

The weather has been toggling between springlike during the day and bitter after sundown; so by the time I go out that night, bottle in hand, the exterior stairs are so icy I have to go down them turned sideways. I knock on Autumn's door, which she opens a full minute later, wearing some kind of kimono over sweats and regarding me only with annoyance, no curiosity at all, despite the fact that I have never done this before.

"Came to ask you something," I say and wave the bottle back and forth in front of my face.

She looks at it and turns and walks back in the direction of her kitchen. That, I realize, is an invitation, or at least as close to one as I'm likely to get from her. I ascend one step from the vestibule area into the kitchen and, just like that, I am in Autumn's home, across the real threshold, for the first time in the eight months of our relationship. I don't know what I was expecting, but I find myself registering a lot of things I didn't expect, for instance the fact that it is very clean. She herself still looks like hell, but somebody sweeps this floor, somebody wipes the counters and the chrome around the sink. And there are photos everywhere, framed photos. Some of Autumn when she was younger and more conventionally alluring, some of an older woman who I guess is her mother, many of random adults and small children in large gatherings, like the kind of posed photos you'd take at a family reunion. I don't know why I'm surprised by this. I don't know why I assumed that she would refuse, even in private, to indulge in sentiment.

She closes the fridge door and sits at the small Formica kitchen table with a bottle of Diet Coke. I can see that she is already a little drunk. At the table is one glass. She does not produce a second one. She pours the soda into her glass until it's about a third full.

"Fill that up," she says to me. "Then when it's empty you can ask me whatever you wanted to ask me."

I unscrew the top, then hesitate. "I'm not just going to sit here silently like a dog, though," I say. "Tell you what. I'll ask you other stuff. Then when you're done I'll ask you what I came here to ask you."

She shrugs and taps the glass impatiently until I start pouring.

"Where'd you go?" I say. "Over the, over the holidays?"

"None of your fucking business," she says. "I have to keep you, what do you call, abreast, of my movements? Just because we live in the same house doesn't give you rights to me, though I know that's what you want."

"What's what I want?"

"To get in here. To hit this. To tap this, although I'm sure I'm a little old for you, by like twenty years."

She takes a drink. It's true that I am conscious of a sexual energy when I'm near her, but that energy comes from her, not me; and it's not about attraction but its opposite. That is, she uses that energy to intimidate and demean me, to push me down. I really don't appreciate it. And maybe it's that, combined with this heady proximity to her—her magnificent self-regard, her mild odor, her open lack of respect for me—but the fact that I don't much like her, right now, is driving an odd urge. To make her show herself to me. So she was right about this much, about me, all along.

"Who are the people in this photo?" I ask her, picking up a frame from the counter behind me. It was taken in somebody's backyard, during what looks like a barbecue. There is a child in the photo, only one among six or eight adults, but the child is wearing a party hat.

"Put that down," she says.

"Cute kid," I say.

She stares at me. Then she picks up her glass and drains it. "Ask me what you wanted to ask me," she says, "and then get the fuck out of here."

"So that thing where you came up and tried to retroactively raise my rent," I say. "I think it's better, going forward, if you and I are honest with each other, or at least a little more honest than we have been. You know I'm on the run. You know I'm hiding. When you were away, the cops came by, some asshole from the power company came by, came upstairs and knocked on my door. I cannot have that. So I'm not trying to be invasive or anything, it's just that I need some stability here, so if you need money, just ask me for it is what I came here to say. You don't need to try to trick me or intimidate me or anything like that. You seem like you're struggling a little bit. So do you need any money is what I came down here to ask."

She stares at me. "You are the cuck of all time," she says. "No, I don't need your fucking help. If I need anything from you I will let— Actually, no, I won't let you know. If I need anything from you I'll take it."

"Okay then," I say. "It was worth a try. I'll leave the bottle. I can't drink that fucking garbage any—"

"You want to get in here," she says, "you come correct. You tell me who you really are and what you've done. Then we'll see. Then we'll see. But don't come around here with your Good Samaritan cosplay bullshit. Don't use me to pretend. You know you can't pretend with me."

Upstairs, everything is different. The house is like a heart beating, a nerve thrumming. I can't see her, but I feel her presence on every surface, in the air. And okay, I more or less drift into some fantasies about her. They are not the type of fantasies I usually have.

I WENT TO that refugee center on Laurel, the one that was in the paper because refugees were afraid to go there. I thought I could volunteer. Volunteer to do what? I don't know. Does it matter? The story mentioned adults taking English classes. I speak English. I could teach someone else how to do it. But of course the first thing they want to do, for some unknown fucking reason, is run a background check on you. Government money, government rules. "All I need is your social," the nice white lady with the gray hair said to me. Bye.

Late March and only mysteriously hardy crusts of snow remain. The trees are bare, but the grass is bright green. Mud everywhere.

And then one afternoon I hear a car idling outside; a young man, wreathed in exhaust, leans deep into the trunk of his car and pulls out an armful of signs. The cheap kind, with two wires that stick in the ground supporting a cardboard image—political signs, urging me to vote for someone, based on their friendly face I guess. There's a local election coming up, in May or June, I don't know. School board, family court judge, things like that. I guess this young party operative was given this task a while ago and has been waiting for the ground to soften. He presses down on each end of the sign to drive it into the muddy strip of earth between the sidewalk and the street, takes the remaining signs and moves down the block. About half an hour later, after his car is gone, I hear Autumn's door bang; she walks out to the end of her yard, yanks the signs there out of the ground, throws them into the street, and goes back inside.

The library books, the ones still there, are such crap. Two entire shelves of James Patterson, but if you want to look for, say, Balzac, who wrote a stupefying amount in his day, too, tough luck.

What are books anyway, though, in this world? Little antiquities. A library is a sort of roadside museum.

Sometimes I sit in one of the leather armchairs and reflect, which is tricky, because you can't fall asleep in there, tempting as that is, what with the warmth and the silence and the luxuriousness of the chairs. If you fall asleep in the library, looking like I look now, the librarian calls a security officer who escorts you right out into the street. I've seen it happen.

The wiry boy, Haji's buddy, the gymnastic one: maybe fourteen, though he looks younger, shorter anyway. He was trying to impress the girls again—the same girls he walks with every day, you'd think the hope of impressing them would have dimmed by now—and he jumped up to one of the higher branches on the low-slung tree like it was a trapeze or the bottom rung of a fire escape. He swung back and forth, arms extended. The girls kept walking without looking back. He swung his torso backward so he could pull up his legs, wrap his knees around the branch, and hang that way. The girls were by now out of view. He grabbed the branch with his hands again and started to swing back and forth, knees bent, to develop enough momentum to go all the way around, three hundred and sixty degrees. He was his own audience now, or so he believed. And he did it! He made the full circle and gave a little exclamation of surprise and pleasure—at least I thought I heard that—and then he wound himself up and went around again and just at the apex of his feet, just when his head was the part of him closest to the ground, the limb snapped, and he fell.

Right on his head. Not on the pavement, though he only missed it by a foot, on the grass. The girls were gone. The block was empty. A great deal of uncertainty, at that moment, as to what to do.

Best estimate, retrospectively: twenty seconds before he stirred. Maybe he lost consciousness. No way of knowing. He stood and looked up the block and down it. He rubbed his neck. His jacket, a thin green fatigue jacket with eccentrically placed zippers, had dirt all over it and a rip at the elbow and he looked at that rip a long time. Then he trudged off to school, looking broken, all the bounce gone from his step. The physical pain would wear off quickly at that age.

But then eight hours later, as the children flow by left to right, every single one of them pauses to stare at the broken limb still lying across the sidewalk. They regard it as if it were a meteor, as if it had fallen not five feet but from somewhere previously invisible to them. They don't touch it. They seem to be arguing about it; the desire to overhear them is countered by the fear of the noise the window would make if opened farther. The wiry boy himself never appears. Probably took a different route home today.

Two or three hours after that, a string of oaths reaches me through my cracked-open window. On the sidewalk, Autumn stands astride the huge broken limb and stares up and down the street with her hands on her head. She looks angry. She also looks a little unsteady on her feet. Abruptly, she spins around and stares in the direction of my window; I drop to the floor, maybe fast enough, maybe not. After a while she goes back inside and slams her door.

Through the floor, that night, her voice, sometimes quite loud and angry, sometimes softer, at one point almost weepy. There is no car in the driveway, and I don't hear any voice down there other than hers. It's possible that she is talking on the phone.

Monday morning comes and goes and the limb just sits there. The garbage collectors don't touch it. It's eight or nine feet long.

Which means the boy must walk past it. He does so quickly, without looking at it or breaking stride, but the others must know what's happened somehow, because their hooting is merciless. Even the girls point at it—and at him—and laugh. Is there any reason to expect poor children, refugee children, to be any kinder in spirit, any less savage and hurtful than children of greater advantage? No, there is not. Joining in the laughter at his own expense might be the boy's best strategy, but he doesn't, he can't. Maybe he can't forgive himself for being so scared in the moment, even though no one else witnessed it, not as far as he knows. More likely he is just humbled by having failed at the perfectly pointless and arbitrary physical test that he spontaneously designed for himself. Anyway, he looks miserable. He wears a hat, which may or may not conceal a bandage of some kind.

Monday afternoon, I hear the children's voices again and then, from downstairs, the bang of a door being pushed open.

"Hey!" Autumn's voice rings out. She is walking in a straight line through the muddy, overgrown yard. The children have frozen in place, not in fear exactly but just because hers is a commanding presence. She stops halfway. I think it is so she can continue to yell.

"Which one of you little fuckers vandalized my cherry tree?" she says.

They look only at her, not at each other. Nor, as I am afraid will happen, do they look up at my window. I am trying to conceal myself behind the thin curtain.

"You know that word? Van-da-lize? That's a priceless fucking tree, and it's mine, this is my property, and you just ruined it, what, just to be assholes?"

They all know who damaged it; he is standing right there. But they are impressively stoic. They seem to have decided to let this storm break over them.

"Let me give you an American civics lesson, you little ingrates," she says. She must be audible up and down the whole block. "You ever heard of Stand Your Ground? Well, this is my fucking ground. Vandalizing my ground equals stealing from me. It's a crime, and you commit a crime here, you and your whole fucking immigrant family go back to wherever you came from. Understand me? One phone call, that's all it takes, and it's back on the fucking boat for you."

She sounds healthy, I'll say that for her. Stronger than I've seen her since she came back from wherever she went.

"And I'm not the only eyes on you either," she says—and then, horrifyingly, she turns around, her back to them, and points up at my window. I step aside and flatten my back against the wall like I was in a gunfight. "Isn't that right? My tenant is up there. He's watching. He watches you all the fucking time, don't you, you pervert? He lives here too. You do something wrong, he'll know!"

Is it really about the tree—that is, do I find it plausible that Autumn is roused to action by the marred beauty of a cherry tree? Maybe. Even hateful people are not impervious to beauty. The one doesn't cancel out the other. More likely, though, what matters to her is simply the idea that it's hers and not theirs, which is assuming it's legally hers at all. It does look like hell now. Asymmetrical and wounded. The huge limb lies beneath it, across the sidewalk; the children hop over it without slowing down.

I wake up from a nap—not even really sure what time it is, other than afternoon, because the house itself is casting a shadow in front of me—and someone has come along and hammered a bunch of new campaign signs into the grass between the sidewalk and the street. So-and-so for comptroller, so-and-so for city council, so-and-so for district attorney. A piece of durable cardboard, printed in color, double-sided on a thin wire frame, jammed into the ground so that the sign itself is only a few inches higher than the grass. They're quite colorful, like flags except they don't move, and their messaging is a bit on the brute-force side, which is to say that there is no messaging at all, only the name, an effort to drive the name deep enough into your head that you will pull the lever beside it when you see it, without thinking, like a rat in expectation of a treat. Even the candidate's party affiliation is not printed, though sometimes the colors themselves are a clue to that—again, working subliminally, trying to get you to act without knowing why.

There's one sign that's slightly different, though—this one posted directly across the street, thus in full, billboard-like view from my window. It's for a candidate for city court judge, whose real name is unusual enough to constitute an identifying detail so I will make one up: Hubert. It's larger and higher off the ground than the others—large enough that its sawhorse-shaped frame is made of wood rather than simple wire—and it features a photo of him. He's not alone in that, but while the other candidate photos are simple, smiling headshots, in this photo Judge Hubert is in a desert, in full camo, helmet off, smiling at the camera, standing beside the open turret of a tank. He's a handsome fellow and buff too. A vet, it seems. No way of telling how long ago the picture was taken. Maybe in his distant youth, maybe last year, maybe yesterday. There's always a war in the sand somewhere.

Who would vote for a judge in a tank? What's the think-ing there? "Appeal this, motherfucker"? He'll probably win; his ad budget is manifestly bigger than anyone else's. Not my problem, though. Voting, elections, that's all over for me. I won't miss it. Talk about deck chairs on the *Titanic*.

At dusk, Autumn walks calmly out her front door, ciga-rette stuck in her mouth, and throws all the signs into the street again, the ones on her side anyway. The judge and his tank still gaze confidently from the other side of the road. It's not her property over there, technically, and that wooden rig looks too heavy to move without help.

A few mornings later, I listen to the radio for a while, news of the world, volume lowered to a mumble. I make a cup of coffee in the little French press I bought at a tag sale, I go to the front window to open the curtain and let in some light, and there is a second limb, not quite as large, on the ground beneath the cherry tree. You can see the saw mark, bright and tan, near the trunk. I swear I never heard a thing.

THE POLICE come again, no lights this time—it's the middle of the afternoon—but my heart is jolted by the crackle of radio static. Unacceptable. I am sitting in my bathroom on the closed toilet holding my breath when I realize I haven't heard that crackling noise in a few minutes now, and when I venture out to the front window I can see that the patrol car is gone. The relief I feel makes me jump even higher when, behind me, there is a knock on my door.

"I'm not coming in," Autumn says. While she talks she is staring at the eye level deadbolt I installed on the door months ago. It's possible she's never noticed it before. "Just wanted you to know that I tried to get them to interview you, but he said no need. He was a sarcastic little bitch about the whole thing, to be honest. Kept asking if I'd really called 911 about a tree, which obviously I did, he knew that. Serves me right for calling a cop in the first place. God, I fucking hate cops. Well, I don't mind going next level if I have to. Stand my fucking ground. Listen, I never asked you. You didn't see anything, did you?"

"No," I say.

"Liar," she says. "Why you want to protect these little illegals I don't know. Don't you remember being a kid? Kids

113

are horrible, and these are the worst of the worst. Don't let me find out you're protecting them."

Her hair's in a ponytail, which frankly is a much better look for her than the usual sloppy bun. She has given herself some sort of manicure.

"No," I say. "How would I even do that?"

"Anyway, one thing I can tell you, they're cleaning that shit up. Those kids. They trespass on my property, and I can't get the cops interested in that but fuck if I'm going out there and cleaning up after them. I promise you I can speak a language there that every one of those little foreign fuckers will understand." She turns and energetically descends the stairs. One thing I've learned about her: she never says hello or goodbye.

She has a gun. That's what that stand-my-ground nonsense is about. Once it dawns on me, I'm sure of it. She's exactly the sort of person who would own at least one gun, "for protection," and you can't necessarily blame her, a woman living alone in her own house in a neighborhood like this.

The severed limbs look more and more dead; they turn incrementally brittle while everything around them greens. If I can see them out my window, Autumn can see them out her window, and of course the kids pass them twice every weekday. In their deadness, they are provocative. Something is going to happen if I don't intervene but on whose side?

I'm not anybody's ally in this, and I don't particularly want to be.

I want peace. A just and lasting peace, peace in our time. I've always wanted peace, and I used to imagine that made me some kind of radical. But now I get it that peace is self-serving; peace protects the status quo and those who like it.

When I get to the library I see with a start that all but two of the club chairs in Periodicals are gone. The librarian sees me looking over my shoulder, trying to remember how many chairs were there before, and says, before I can ask: "To discourage vagrancy."

"I was wondering," I say with maximum meekness, "if there's any sort of printed directory or list of city services."

It's clear from her expression that she misunderstands.

"Not social services, municipal services," I say. "Like schedules for trash pickup, that kind of thing."

"Online," she says. "All that information is online," and she gives me the .gov address. "If you want, I can sign you up for one of the terminals. Half-hour limit if anyone's waiting."

"No thank you," I say quickly, wanting to cut that conversation short before it gets to a request for ID. "Nothing in print, then," I say. She shakes her head, and I give her a comic shrug and turn away.

And then the Black man in the polo shirt buttoned up to the neck, the same guy who's always there, leans toward me, over the arm of one of the two remaining chairs. He says if I tell him what I want to look up, he'll look it up for me. When I give him the request, his eyes widen and he laughs. "Man, if I'd known it was that boring, I would have kept my mouth shut," he says. "Too late now."

Yard refuse is picked up only on the last Monday of every month. The pieces must be no longer than two and a half feet in length and stacked neatly, not bagged, with the exception of mown grass, raked leaves, and Christmas trees, which must be bagged. He wrote it down for me, in a visibly shaking hand. His name is Oscar. He is nosy. "What you want to know all this for?" he says.

That indie hardware store, Feeney's, where I bought the deadbolt kit? Gone. Out of business. I know where there's a True Value, and a Home Depot, and an Ace. But I won't go in there. That is, there's got to be a way to avoid going in there. Extremely unlikely that the Goodwill would ever have a saw—who would donate a saw?—but I ask them anyway if such a thing ever comes in. "No weapons" is the rote answer.

Time is a factor and I have no other ideas: I ask Oscar if he knows a good place to buy tools that's not Home Depot or the like. I have prepared an answer for when he asks me what I've got against Home Depot, but instead he asks, "What tools you need?" A saw, I say, like a hacksaw, for tree work. "I got a pruning saw," he says. He'll even deliver it to me if I'll tell him where I live. I say he shouldn't go to such trouble; he can just bring it to the library and I'll meet him outside. He appears hurt by this but agrees. When he hands over the saw the next day, it looks suspiciously unused. I promise to return it tomorrow, and he just shakes his head and laughs and turns without a word to enter the library, where, armed now with a saw, I cannot follow him.

It's a total of seven cuts. Exhausted, I put the nine pieces in a pyramid on the edge of the grass just beside where the trash bins go on pickup day. My back feels like it's on fire. I turn to look at Autumn's windows; all the lights are out, but it's impossible to conclude for sure that she's not in there.

If she confronts me, I will tell her that it was a matter of self-interest, that I couldn't have the cops coming around here anymore. I can't permit any confrontation that might draw me in. She won't like that, but she will understand it.

How to be invisible when you are walking down a crowded city sidewalk on a sunny day past homes and stores and you are carrying a large saw? There's no way to normalize it. Everyone stares at me. I have not thought this out very well, or at all really. If Oscar is not at the library, I will have to turn around and go home. He's usually there this time of day. Still, they are not going to let me stroll into the library holding a saw. So what am I going to do? Stand outside the windows and wave it at him? That turns out to be exactly what I do. He looks at me in astonishment; I try, with a sort of sheepish smile, to make it seem like this is in any way a normal sort of interaction.

He puts on his coat, his hat, rather unhurriedly in my opinion, and meets me out on the sidewalk.

"So, thank you for this," I say. "It really did the trick."

He doesn't take it from me, only looks at me quizzically.

"Are you crazy?" he says, though his tone is not angry. "What am I supposed to do with that?" He is careful not to look at it, even while referring to it. "You couldn't put it in a bag or something?"

A fair point, though I'm not sure a saw wrapped in a white plastic trash bag would have looked less ominous.

Oscar shakes his head. "A Black man, in this city, walking into a public library carrying a saw," he says.

I try holding the saw flat against my leg so that it's not as visible. The effect, Oscar's look tells me, is absurd.

"I have a pen," he says. "Do you have a piece of paper, anything, maybe like an old receipt in your wallet?"

"No," I say.

"You don't even want to look?"

"No," I say, "I don't have a wallet."

He shakes his head. "What's your address?" he says. And I am so cowed and nervous at this point that I give it to him.

"I'll be there at three," he says, and he turns and walks back inside. I take the saw back home, this time holding it casually, swinging it a little even, though the expression on my face is probably not all that convincing.

At ten minutes to three I put the saw in a trash bag and take it out to the sidewalk. I am praying that he will not be late, because if he is then we will risk being out there when the students flow home from school. But I can't wait inside. I never mentioned anything about the separate entrances so he would knock on Autumn's door for sure.

He is on time. Men who wear their shirts buttoned all the way to the neck are not likely to run late, I suppose. He's back to his usual demeanor, like we are great friends, like everything about me is his business. "This your house?" he says. "It's nice!"

He reasonably expects to be invited in. "No," I say, "I just rent a room here." I point to the window and instantly regret it. I'm just trying to explain what would otherwise read as an aggressive lack of politeness or gratitude. The fact that he's Black and I am white is certainly part of my fear of being misread.

He nods and looks down at the wood pyramid a few feet away. I can hear distant, loud voices, high voices, on the street behind me. "So you just doing some yard work," Oscar says, "to help out?"

"Something like that, yeah."

"Get a break on the rent?"

The voices are getting louder, and I am afraid to turn around. "Listen," I say. "I don't want to be rude, but I have to go. I'm so grateful for your lending me the saw. It really helped me out. With my landlord. So thanks."

His face clouds. There is no way to explain to him what is happening, but in the absence of that explanation, a familiar mistrust takes hold. "Yeah, okay," he says, in a new tone. "Well, maybe I'll see you."

"Sure. Tougher since they took all the chairs out of the library, though. That seemed kind of unwelcoming. Why would they do that?"

"Yeah, well, always a chair for a white man. Though you might try dressing better. Anyway, now I know where you live, right? In case I ever need my favor returned." And he takes the bag from my hand and walks away. I feel relieved and also guilty but right behind that guilt is a kind of hot defensiveness, like fine, fuck you, I was never the one looking for a buddy anyway. "Excuse me," says a polite voice, and a girl passes me from behind as I stare down Sugar Street. Head down, I cross the lawn toward the exterior stairs, trying not to run.

That night—quite late, late enough that I'm lying in bed with the lights off, though sleep seems unlikely—I hear steps on the stairs. I brace for a knock, but instead I hear the swish of a piece of paper sliding under the door. After the steps recede, I get up and unfold it. The light from the street is enough to read by, and my eyes are adjusted to the dark. It's just handwriting on a plain piece of paper, like from a computer printer. "You are the cuck of all time," it reads. "I want you out."

TWO STRAIGHT DAYS of pouring rain. The kids walk past anyway, same as ever, only silently.

I don't own a scale, but I know I've lost weight; clothes I bought just this fall fit differently now. About six weeks ago I gave myself a haircut. Maybe that was too paranoid of me. I probably could have risked entering a damn barbershop. The interesting thing is not that my appearance is degrading but that my inner life may be degrading to fit my outward appearance.

I haven't seen her in a few days; I'm not sure she's even left the house. She hasn't had a shift in quite a long time, as far as I know. She may not be working at all anymore. It's not that hard to imagine a scenario wherein she doesn't remember leaving me that note at all.

Still, it seems smartest to tread extra lightly for a while. When she's home, I know she's home, and I'm sure the same goes for her too. There seems something provocative about me now, about knowing I am there under her roof, no matter how quiet and invisible. So I try to get out a little more during the day, for both our sakes.

One night she brought a man home with her. I heard their voices, but by the time I got to the window they were inside. Laughter audible through the register, then silence, and then it was showtime. Which is to say she is loud, this Autumn, rather spectacularly loud. Good for her. Not every exclamation had the ring of absolute authenticity, though perhaps this is ungenerous, perhaps it's not fair to judge through heat registers, through floorboards. And anyway, why shouldn't she make this man, whoever he was, feel good about himself in this way? It seemed quite giving on her part.

But I lay awake for hours after they'd stopped, in the grip of a fantasy that she had seduced this man in order to get him to come upstairs and beat the shit out of me, kick me out, throw my stuff in the street. In exchange for her doing whatever he wanted. Dumb, B-movie thoughts, but in the dark it was plausible enough for me to get up and double-check the locks on the door.

A look at him, though not a clear one, in the soft morning light. Not a bruiser by any means. He wore a suit and a baseball cap. He walked by himself out to the curb and rocked back and forth on his heels until a cab came and got him.

The wiry boy walks by, in his usual group, with one of those tiny bottles labeled 5-Hour Energy or some such corporate poison. He drains it in one gulp and then, with perfect lack of affect, without a glance or a hitch in his stride, he tosses the tiny empty bottle with his right hand across the left side of his body; it arcs through the air and onto Autumn's lawn.

What does it matter? What could this grubby, weedy, uneven, unfenced patch of ground cover mean to anybody? But it is contested space now, and if there is anything human beings can't resist it is an utterly pointless contest. I go out there and pick it up, not looking behind me at Autumn's windows.

Not sleeping well. I don't like being in the house, but I don't like being away from it either. I pulled up a linoleum square, but the envelope is still too thick to fit under it without creating an immediately noticeable lump.

The REELECT JUDGE HUBERT signs are all over the place now, gun turrets looming over the flimsy cardboard faces of rivals and ticket-sharers alike. There's one downtown, on the edge of the plaza with the drained skating rink. I find a shady spot and watch the kids cavort, though I try not to look like I'm watching them, because everyone thinks everyone else is a pedophile these days. And since I am unaccompanied and don't exactly look like I'm on lunch hour from my office job, my presence, if noticed at all, is suspicious. Still, I feel, at long last, a little safer in outdoor settings like this, like if anything were going to happen it would have happened by now. Life in the commercial hub is busy and varied enough to incorporate me. It's fine, there are places to sit, it's cool in the shade, I feel unseen.

And then—not asleep but apparently in enough of a daze that I don't see it coming—I am poked roughly by a cop.

"Can't sleep here," he says, though I was never sleeping. He has red hair, cut very short, and his skin is patchy, like the sun is getting to him. He has poked me with the end of some kind of hard silicone baton. He wears a short-sleeved patrolman's uniform, with the city crest on it. Around his waist, the medieval-looking belt that holds the gun, the handcuffs, the pepper spray, the radio. No taser. Not in the budget, I imagine.

"You have to move it along, sir," he says, with that military sort of politeness. "Let's go."

"Why?" I say. "Aren't these public benches?"

He looks at me incredulously. "I'm sorry, what?" he says. Before I can repeat my point, he wedges the baton under my armpit and tries to lift me with it. He considers me untouchable, I realize; that is what all the weapons are for.

"Stop it," I say. I am shocked to hear myself say it. I've never been in this position before, but I am not thinking at all, I am in the realm of reaction. I do refrain from grabbing the stick itself; that would too clearly give him the type of excuse he's looking for. I stand up. He smiles, and then he puts his face unnecessarily close to mine.

"Let's keep this nice, sir," he says, in a confidential tone. "There are all these mommies and children around."

Indeed there are people watching now, some discreetly and some eagerly.

"Why do I have to move? This is a public space."

"Why? Did you just ask me why? What is your name?"

"Hank Thoreau," I say.

"Do you have an address?"

I nod.

"What is it?"

There is no way I am giving a police officer my address. I give him a fake one, on a street in Stone Farms.

"Go there right now, and don't let me ever see you here again," he says.

"You haven't told me what I'm doing that's illegal," I say.

He takes the cuffs off his belt. I move a step backward, out of his reach.

"Okay, okay," I say. "I'm going. It'd be nice if you could tell me what I was doing that's illegal, though."

"Just trying to protect decent people," he says malevolently and smiles.

And I walk home, fuming, fantasizing, looking behind me occasionally to make sure he isn't following.

I know, *I know*, it is the whitest thing ever, being shocked and upset by the lack of respect displayed toward me by a police officer. What, did I think I was going to change his mind? There was no victory to be had in that confrontation, and so I should have just avoided it entirely. I should have moved off silently when he told me to. I took a huge risk in talking back to him, a stupid risk. He had the cuffs in his hand. Had the moment ratcheted up just one more tick, I'd be in jail now and this whole last year would be for naught, my life—both the old one and the new one—would be over. Where does it come from, that barren outrage, that hot belief in the rules? Telling yourself not to feel it is about as effective as trying to halt the blood in your veins.

A quick story from my old life: one night I woke from a dream that I'd heard a knock on the door, only it wasn't a dream, because I heard the knock again. I looked out the bedroom window and saw a police light turning in my driveway. I'll never forget that walk to the door, going over, in my head, the whereabouts of everyone important to me, trying to figure out which one the cops had come to inform me was dead.

But instead it was a young officer, very young, informing me that he and his partner had apprehended a man trying to break into my garage. He pointed to where the man sat in the back of the squad car; I couldn't really see him. There had been a rash of such break-ins around the neighborhood, the officer told me—I remember specifically he used the word "rash"—and they could arrest this man only if I agreed to press charges. Otherwise they would let him go. The officer would write up the statement, and I would just have to sign it.

I agreed. It was a hot night, and I stood in my driveway in my pajamas while the officer went back to the car and wrote up the statement, which was just a few lines long. I could see the man's head in silhouette in the back seat, held high, facing forward, not moving. But here is the part of the story that sticks with me: after I signed, and the business of our encounter was over, the officer's demeanor changed, his air of authority was set aside. "You know what," he said and smiled. "When I was in high school, I worked summers with a landscaping crew, and I remember this house. I used to mow this lawn. They wouldn't let me trim hedges or anything like that, I was fifteen, they didn't want me to ruin anything. But I remember this lawn."

I think it's safe to recount that story, because it offers no identifying details. Plus, pretty much every white man of a certain social stratum must have a story resembling that one.

I WON'T GO BACK to the library anymore, just because of the awkwardness with that Oscar guy, the way he pushed too hard and then acted all hurt, the misinterpreted racial dynamic there, which, I know from experience, gets messier the more you try to clear it up. Also the fact that the library took out almost all the chairs. But I find instead a great used bookstore—an enormous place, with CDs and records, too, and there is never anyone in there. How it stays in business, I can't fathom. The owner is always there; he never speaks, but he doesn't make you uncomfortable about staying for hours as long as you buy something in the end, even a little fifty-cent paperback. Easy enough to do. After a while I have a small tower of them on the floor of my room, unread, and I think about searching the Goodwill for some kind of shelf.

Killing an afternoon there, looking through a section labeled Abnormal Psychology (how are you going to resist that?), and I come across some galley or pamphlet titled *The Levenson Test*. It takes me a few seconds to answer the bell that rings: this is the test Autumn mentioned wanting to give me, way back when, the test she mentioned having been given herself. I flip through the pages, but I don't focus on them. I'm thinking instead that this is my in with her; this is my icebreaker. Things have to be set right. We have been avoiding each other. That is, I know I've been avoiding her, and I suspect she's been avoiding me because she knows she'd have to follow through on her threat to evict me, and for whatever reason, she doesn't really want to.

I am still having fantasies about that cop who rousted me when I closed my eyes outdoors. Detailed fantasies: in one I run into him coming out of a bar, drunk and out of uniform, and I punch him in the face over and over until I hear sirens and I run off and leave him in some alley. It's so childish. The last time I punched anyone in the face was elementary school. I'm going to jump a cop now? But I can't turn it off, in my head. There's one where I hit him in the knees with a pipe or a bat. Completely implausible. It's not me. It's in me—I guess that's clear, it's something I would do—but it's not something I could do, lacking the courage, the strength, the technique, lacking all of it, really.

And what did he do to me to merit this fictional revenge beating? He humiliated me. He hurt my pride. He dominated me psychologically. Poor baby.

On that community bulletin board outside the library, a flyer with the words SPEAK YOUR TRUTH in large block letters catches my eye, and I get a little closer:

We will not be silent anymore. We invite you to speak out in solidarity with the people of America who join in uprising and rebellion against homophobia and systemic racism. We will not remain silent any longer as black and brown bodies are abused by the police. As our toothless anger disappears into the echoing hallways of social media and our mounting rage will consume us if we do not release it. We invite you to speak your grief aloud. Speak your truth today. We call upon all the residents of our region, no matter your skin color, your community, or your creed: Do not be silent. Your anger is real. Speak your truth today.

Then there's an address—the parking lot of an art gallery—and a time and a date. The date was five days ago. So I guess all that truth got spoken. And wow, what a difference it made!

I mean, okay, I agree with the bit about the "echoing hallways of social media," though it's a bit preciously put. But deliver me, please, from people "speaking their truth." If truth is that subjective, then it comes down to power or force, and we're all fucked anyway. "We will be silent no longer." When were you silent? In my experience, you won't fucking stop talking. Speech is self-idolizing. Be *more* silent.

And the joke is, a little thing like that, some flyer that wasn't even pushed into my hand but just stuck somewhere I happened to see it, that puts me in a confrontational mood for the rest of the day. I walk around muttering angrily to myself about it. What do I have to be angry about? Still, it's academic to say I'm not entitled to it. It's there. You can fully concede the argument that you aren't entitled to it, but you'll wake up in the morning and it'll still be there.

I have to make it appear casual if I can; knocking on her door would only excite her defensive instincts. Sunday night I take a bag of trash out back and I stand there with it at my feet, hoping no one can see me, for half an hour, maybe more, until I hear her door open. I drop the bag in the garbage can and come around the side of the house, wiping my hands.

"Oh hi," I say. "Need any help?"

She is holding one trash bag by its red plastic handles. "Got it, thanks," she says and squeezes past me.

"Hey," I say, and I can see her back stiffen. "I was thinking, remember that time you wanted to give me that personality test? Because you thought I was a sociopath?"

She stops. "Psychopath," she says. "Levenson test."

"Yeah. Well, I got a copy and if you want, I could come down and you could give that to me, just to put your mind at ease. I mean I thought about it, and I don't like the idea of you thinking you've got a psychopath sleeping upstairs from you every night."

The look on her face is not concern so much as revulsion. There seems nothing about me she doesn't find subpar. But she doesn't say no. She doesn't say anything, just dumps her garbage on top of my garbage and reenters her home.

It's a risk, but I feel like I have to at least try to do something to change the downhill run of her thoughts about me. That Fireball stuff—the whiskey that makes your throat burn—her eyes light up when she sees it, and I feel proud of myself for having figured her out even to that small extent.

First we get drunk, in nearly complete silence. After avoiding my eyes for the first few drinks she starts staring at me like she wants me to go.

"Can we maybe sit in your living room?" I say. "It's hot in here, and these little chairs are rough on my back. I can see from here that you have real chairs in the living room."

"No," she says. "Nice try. First it's the chairs, then the couch, then why don't we just move to the bed. I know what you want, and you ain't getting it. Look at your face! Is it because I said 'ain't'? You went to college, didn't you, you went to some fancy-ass college."

"If you like," I say. "Sure."

"I went to college, too, you know," she says. "A semester and a half. It was bullshit. The only class I liked was Human Psych. If I'd stuck with it, I'd have gone into that, because I have a very strong natural gift for understanding other people, better than they understand themselves. Diagnosing them. I have a knack for—"

I tap the book, which sits next to the whiskey bottle on the kitchen table. "Wow me," I say. She opens it and flips through it. Without looking up, she taps her nail on the rim of her glass, and I refill it. "Yeah, here it is," she says. "Okay, ready?"

"Let's do it."

"On a scale of one to five: one is strongly disagree, five is strongly agree, three is neutral. 'For me, what's right is whatever I can get away with.'"

"This is a test?"

"A diagnostic test, not the kind of test you can fail. Well, I guess maybe you could fail it actually. Come on, one to five, 'For me, what's right is whatever I can get away with.'"

"One."

"Okay, you're lying, but that's actually baked into the test. But try not to lie. I know that's hard for you. 'I would be upset if my success came at someone else's expense.'"

"How many questions are there?"

"A lot of questions. Okay, you don't like that one? 'I don't plan anything very far in advance.'"

"One is disagree? One."

"'Love is overrated.' Total softball, that one. Shouldn't even be on here. They should have asked me how to give this fucking test."

And then she stops—her whole face, her energy, just stops—like she hears something outside the house. But it's silent. She has gone somewhere in her head.

"Autumn?" I say.

She sees something. It is probably a memory. But in the moment it is much more present than I am. Gently I reach over and slide the textbook away from her. "Here, we can keep going," I say. She is worrying me. I turn the book around toward me.

"'In today's world, I feel justified in doing whatever I can get away with to succeed.' Yikes. 'Success is based on the survival of the fittest; I am not concerned about the losers.' Okay, to be fair that does sound a tiny bit like you, am I right?"

Her eyeballs finally move a little, and then they are back to focusing on me. "No," she says in a small voice. "No you don't. Give me that. Give me that!"

I push the book back toward her.

"I'm Levenson," she says. "Not you."

"Sorry," I say. "Of course. Ask away."

But she doesn't take her eyes off me. She reaches out to grab the edge of the table. "I mean, who are you?" she says. "What are you even doing in my house? How did you get in here? You better not try anything. You better not get any ideas. I have a gun here."

And without leaving her chair, she pulls open a kitchen drawer and produces it.

"Nobody even knows who you are," she says. "If I dropped you right here, nobody would blame me, I'd be justified."

"You're right," I say calmly. "You're totally right. But look, the rent is due again soon, and you want to keep me around at least that long, right?"

She looks at me critically, the way a doctor might look at me. "Nah, you're not so much," she says. "You're just the kind of guy who snaps one day. I can see it. You haven't lived a life of crime, you lived a soft life, it's in your voice, it's written all over your face. You're nothing to worry about. You had, like, one moment of courage, and you'll be running from that moment the rest of your life."

A warm night, second week of April. Not late, maybe six thirty. I am having a beer, hearing the faint whine of a power saw in somebody's distant driveway, reduced to a not-unpleasant kind of insect sound by my closed window. Then I hear steps outside. Too light a tread, too fast, to be Autumn. Three knocks, gentle ones, not a pounding like you'd get from law enforcement. I could pretend not to be here—my lights are off—but curiosity wins out.

"Good evening, sir," he says.

It's the boy with the blond fade. This is the first time I've seen him, other than at a distance, since he and his friends hooted me off on the sidewalk when I asked them about Abiha. So, two months? Six weeks? If the high, dyed, asymmetrical hair looked badass before, it's somewhat self-undermining now against the dark V-neck sweater over a collared shirt he has worn in an effort to be formal.

"I'm an eighth grader at Wysocki Middle School, down the street, and we are selling candy to raise money for a class trip," he says. "I have—"

"Again?" I say. "A class trip where?"

He pauses, as if to collect himself. Under the spell, perhaps, of the spiel he has spent so long rehearsing, he shows no sign of recognizing me, of having met me before. "The state capitol," he says.

"Didn't you already go to the state capitol?" I say. He looks confused. "Not you, your class. Didn't somebody else come to my door back in the fall and sell me some candy for a trip to the state capitol back then?"

He doesn't look embarrassed or caught out; he looks as if his feelings are hurt.

"Don't you remember me?" I say.

His mouth drops open as if to speak, but nothing comes out. I try to remind myself that he is just a child, but it's too late for that.

"It's not about the money. It's that I don't like being made a fool of," I say. "If you want to go to the state capitol five times a year, I'm perfectly fine with that, I just don't like being made a fool of."

"I am sorry to disturb you, sir," the boy says. He takes a step backward, half turning in the direction of the stairs.

"And I love candy," I say. "I really do. If I could just get you to be honest with me, if you would just show me that much respect, I might buy all your candy. How much have you got in there?"

Kids in groups are dissemblers, but he is alone with me, and his eyes tell me that he is scared in a way I don't think he would be if he remembered me, if he remembered having met me before. It is confounding that I have left this faint an impression on him. Well, I will make myself memorable.

"Open it up," I say. "Seriously. What would it cost me to buy the whole case?"

Slowly, he gets down on one knee and lays the red plastic case—just like Haji's, maybe the very same one—on the landing outside my open front door. He lifts the lid. The trouble he is having in counting up his inventory is that he is trying to do so without taking his eyes off me.

"What was your favorite part of the state capitol last time?" I say. "The rotunda, I bet."

Here I am, standing there, the kid kneeling in front of me. It's all come to this. Whatever pits us against each other, whatever dooms us in our lizard brains, whatever makes the world the unredeemable pit that it is and will always be: here it is, in this moment. It was never not here. It will be here until we finish wiping each other off the earth.

I turn around and—closing the door almost all the way, but not latching it, in order to make him stay—I go under the futon for the envelope. I unwind the string and open it up and I count out five thousand dollars. It takes a minute. When I pull the door wide again he is still on his knees, lips moving, running his fingers over the candy bars. He's had plenty of time; he must have been nervous and started over.

"Stand up," I say. I'm trying to make my voice gentle, but I can't quite do it. He stands up and sees the money and his eyes go very wide. I hold it out to him.

"Just take it," I say. "It's not a trick. I mean it, take it."

He takes it without looking directly at it. "I don't . . ." he says.

"Just one thing I want to ask you," I say. "Where's Abiha?"

"Abiha?"

"Your friend. Abiha. She was here and then all of a sudden she wasn't. Does she still go to Wysocki?"

And with the mention of her name, I can see in his eyes that he remembers me now. "I don't know, sir," he says.

"You don't have to sir me. Just tell me what happened to her. Where is she?"

"I don't know who she is."

"I don't mean 'where is she' like I'm going to go find her, I mean what happened to her. Is she okay?"

"I don't know," he says. "I don't know who that is. It's a big school. I really don't."

"Cops, immigration, maybe her family? Maybe they just moved, mom or dad got a job somewhere or something? You can tell me! There's nothing I could do about it anyway!"

He is trying not to cry.

"Put the money in your pocket," I say. "Someone might be watching."

He does it. He is too confused to be grateful.

"Goodnight," I say. I start to close the door.

"Wait," he says. "Don't you still want the candy?"

I do. I do want the candy. It's only fair. I reach across the threshold; he puts the handle of the plastic briefcase in my hand, our fingers brushing uncomfortably, unavoidably, and I shut my door.

$154,010.

Some kind of confrontation is in the air, or maybe under the earth, in any event not making its approach through the usual sensory channels. More demonstrations in the city, as the weather gets warmer. Marches, happenings. It does feel like something is happening, but maybe not what they think is happening. I mean, "change" can mean a lot of things.

A beautiful, sunny afternoon and on the way home from school they loiter in front of the house, talking. A couple of them sit on the remaining lower branch of the cherry tree, keeping a wary eye on the front door while pretending not to. They do not throw anything or discard anything. Eventually they start to move again, left to right across the space framed by the window. But then one of them—a girl, she's there every day, nothing remarkable about her—stops, looks up at the house, and waves to me in the upstairs window, even though I'm sure she can't see me. Then she laughs and trots to join the others.

The school is two and a half blocks away, down Sugar and then left on Oak. On Sunday, of course, no one is there; the doors are locked tight, no possibility of getting inside, and even the first-floor windows are too high off the ground for me to see through. But at least I don't have to worry about being seen, and anyway one can guess at the state of the classrooms from the unbeautiful exterior of the building itself. It is not decrepit by any means. Maybe thirty or forty years old at the most? But it is massive. Brightly lit, even on a day when no one is there. Two long stories. An all-purpose athletic field in front of it, precipitously close to the road. Two sets of clear plexiglass doors at the entrance, one just eight or ten feet beyond the other.

All I can really see is what's visible through the entrance. Wysocki, in big letters over the inner set of doors. I cup my hands around my eyes and press my face to the glass. Metal detectors and a security desk, rows of lockers, various signs and flags reflected off the heavy wax on the floor. A message painted on the wall above the lockers: YOUR ATTITUDE DETERMINES YOUR DIRECTION. No sort of portrait or plaque that might tell me who this Wysocki person was or why this human warehouse should be his legacy. The ethnicity of the name itself says a lot, actually, and not in a good way. Now all the city's Wysockis have moved away and their memorial is this hulk that looks like stock footage from a story about a school shooting. Talk about your end of empire.

Flyers on lampposts, in windows, on the boards nailed over windows. It starts to feel like they're picking up on some unease, some tension in me, rather than the other way around.

All this despite the fact that I have stopped listening to the radio, I have stopped buying the newspaper. None of that interests me anymore. It's a kind of death, or feels like it; my interests are like a closing iris.

But I come home from the park one afternoon and someone has slid a flyer under my door. At the bottom I recognize that graffiti-style FIGHT logo from the piece of paper the young woman pressed in my hand a couple of months ago at the site of the fire. There is to be a silent vigil outside a federal holding facility more or less in the heart of downtown to protest deportation proceedings against several local families. The families are named. One of the last names is the girl Abiha's last name, which I read on the front cover of her notebook. It's a very common last name. Her family is not necessarily the one being referenced.

I have not seen the boy with the blond fade for many days. I have to believe it is because he is taking another route to school. I have poisoned this one for him. But how does he explain it to his friends? Does he lie or tell them the truth? I think he lies. If no one knows he has the money, then no one will ask him for any of it. The only one who knows his secret is me, which would explain why he doesn't want to pass beneath my window. Just from the standpoint of conscience, of personal ease, he would probably prefer it if I were erased from this place, if my existence could go magically unnoticed. Join the club.

To lighten my footprint, going forward. To leave as illegible a mark as possible on the earth, to minimize my use of its resources, not to drain those resources for my comfort. To become unobtrusive, and to live unobtruded upon. To insulate others from all the varieties of damage I can do. Have done. To resist the vanity of thinking that anything I have done can be put right or made better. To see without ruining. To make of my remaining days on earth a kind of spacewalk: to step outside the capsule, to cut the tether. To be blameless. To take no one down with me. To escape surveillance, both targeted and not. To avoid being identified. These, I remind myself, were the goals.

My fridge has stopped working. I hear it running, but nothing in there is cold. What am I going to do, complain to the landlord about it? Fortunately I still have about a month's supply of candy.

I decide that a silent vigil is an idea I can get behind. Not that I'll participate, of course. But in the end, no one would care about your stupid chants or speeches anyway. In the end, your best hope for utility is as a body, one among many. At some point, you are going to be asked to put your body between the state and one of its intended victims. Either you'll do it or you won't. Nothing you express in words in a situation like that will make the slightest difference to anyone.

My room is full of ladybugs. The windows don't seal nearly well enough to keep them out. You feel a little sentimental about them, and then one morning you're awakened by one of them flying into your mouth, and next thing they know it's a killing field.

Sitting on a bench in the park today and a guy comes and sits on the bench next to mine. Which is okay—in fact they're the only two benches on the overlook, the little turnout at the top of the hill that gives the best view of the city and the best breeze as well. A rare, peaceful spot. So this guy, who's not so far below my age, pulls out his phone and starts playing a game, and he leaves the sound up. Five, six feet away from me. Nonstop, irregular beeps and chimes and descending failure sounds.

"Excuse me," I say.

He looks up blankly.

"You know how to mute that thing?" I say.

Nothing.

"Because they have a little button on there, you dumb rude fuck, that silences those noises so that you don't bother

other people around you. That's actually why that button is on there. Can I help you find it?"

I don't know why I went straight there. There were so many other ways to handle it. And he could have kicked my ass if he wanted to, which, in retrospect, it must have sounded a bit like I was asking him to do. I imagine that what stopped him, what frightened him even, was the way I look.

"I mean, do you think that's why I come here?" I went on. There was no one anywhere near us, so no need to keep my voice down. "Because I'm hoping some oblivious asshole will sit down next to me and play his phone in my ear while I take in this lovely view?"

Expressionless, he got up and left. Which in hindsight I respect. But the point of the story is that it's back, that hair trigger, that oversensitivity and outrage, that white-guy pining for escalation despite my having nothing, nothing, with which to back it up.

My deal is that I committed a murder. I did it: I killed a person. Multiple people. I was questioned and arrested and tried, and I was found not guilty. Try living with that! There are people who suspect the truth, and at least one who knows it. But I'm not hiding from anybody; I don't really need to, since I can't be tried again. Think of this as a self-sentencing, then. Internal exile.

My deal is that I am the grandson of one of the five hundred richest people in America. Money has defined me all my life. I don't just mean in the eyes of other people. It's mooted my sense of what's possible; as for my ability to trust, even in my most intimate relationships, that was pretty much strangled in my crib. My grandfather is almost a hundred years old. He won't hang on forever. Legal fights are already brewing in the family over his fortune. Brother against sister, mother against son. I figured out a way to escape all of it. I never actually sold any of the assets in my name; the assets still exist, but the person who owned them does not.

My deal? Long story short, I had a chance to save someone else's life, and I failed. I didn't have the courage. I can't be around the people who know that about me. They will say they have forgiven me, and maybe they have, but forgiving is not the same as forgetting. I need to be forgotten.

My deal was aces over kings. The dealer was a friend of mine, my brother, my cousin, my college roommate. I drew one card and got the third ace. He winked at me; everyone saw, but no one did anything.

It's an ugly city, that's just objective fact. Planned to death, renewed to death; architecturally it's got its little pockets of pleasure but for the most part it's brutalist structures that will never come down, houses that look like they might come down if you blew too hard on them, and Dunkin' Donuts signs. But the people, the human beings—that's where the real ugliness resides. You see it in their faces, especially when they catch you looking. Have they been dehumanized by their surroundings, or have they built a world whose unloveliness has grown over time to reflect their own disregard for it? Well, either way. Industry has fled, the tax base has fled, the city feels like a forest in a drought, one cigarette butt, one unbanked campfire away from inferno. You know how on TV they make a big deal of showing you the first place on earth to hit midnight on New Year's Eve? Tonga, I think it is. This place is like that, except instead of a new year, it's the end of the world.

Sometimes, in my first months here, I felt like a spy, the rush of a secret identity. But I am not a spy. A spy is two people. I'm less than one.

Another Saturday night and I ain't got nobody.

My deal? This is really embarrassing, but I've always wanted to write a novel. Turns out I'm like the princess and the pea in terms of distraction. I need everything perfect, I need all the daily sources of input disconnected. All this is only temporary; when the book's done, I'll go back to my old life. I'm making some decent progress. No, you can't read it yet, but thanks for asking. Maybe when it's done.

THE PLAN was this: More or less in the heart of downtown there is an unmarked building that is used as a federal holding facility for the "processing" and ultimate deportation of those immigrants deemed illegal. A group of citizens was going to stand silently outside this building (there was no way to get any closer to it than the sidewalk) just to mime a kind of collective "we see you." So the protest was symbolic, metaphorical really. We didn't even know for sure that anyone was inside.

I say "we," but I never joined the clot of thirty or forty people or got any nearer to them than a block away. An unmarked federal law enforcement building: are you kidding me? Absolute fucking state of the art surveillance equipment and facial recognition technology. I wore a baseball cap and sunglasses and a bandanna around my neck to pull up over my face if necessary. I watched from across two streets as the group assembled—better view that way anyway. When you're inside a crowd it can seem like a powerful organism but looking from a distance at this collection of mostly middle-aged white women loitering on a downtown sidewalk it didn't exactly register as a game-changing show of power.

Pedestrians who had to step into the street to get around them were silent, too, but scowled or rolled their eyes. One of the problems with a silent vigil, it occurred to me, is how do you know when it's over. After about two hours they were still there, and I started to wonder why I was too.

But then something unexpected happened: the group started moving. Not hurriedly, not like they were being dispersed—no one had come out of the building to acknowledge them at all, much less disperse them—but everyone in the same direction. Right toward me as it happened. I heard one group of women talking animatedly, and I fell in behind them to catch the drift of what was going on.

Somebody somewhere claimed to have gotten a tip via some kind of social media that a raid was scheduled on a particular house in the city that very night; this was partly why there were—or seemed to be—so few people inside the facility right now. Federal immigration agents were coming to arrest and deport the family in that house. It was impossible to verify any of this, but people were acting on the belief that it was true. The new idea was to gather the maximum number of bodies and pack them into the space between the street and this family's front door. There was some uncertainty about whether they had decided to stand or sit. I pulled the bandanna up over my face and followed.

I didn't know who was in that house. I don't know what they'd done or not done to attract the particular attention of immigration authorities. I heard somebody say their kids were teenagers, so it's not impossible that this was the family of one of the kids I saw every day, but it's not likely either. It didn't matter. I wasn't really interested in joining, but I did want to watch it. I respected it. The canny humility of it. No clever signs, no call-and-response, just a lawn or a stoop turned into silent bodies and the decision put before the authorities as to how that expanse of bodies was to be traversed. To reduce yourself to an obstacle, a piece of an obstacle, something for the thoughtless and sadistic to have to hack through, to make it slightly more difficult for them to get where they wanted to go. A stone in their shoe. I liked it.

By the time I got there, people were already seated in loose rows across the small lawn and on the front stoop. They conversed quietly. Whoever was in the house stayed in the house, lights out. I took up a position across the street. No police or other authority was in sight. The sun was starting to go down. Word spread about a store owner two blocks away who was letting people use his bathroom; every once in a while, someone would stand up from the grass and wander off in that direction. Not all of them came back.

When it was fully dark, the cops showed up. City cops, interestingly, lights flashing in silence. They arrived in cars and in vans, probably ten or fifteen of them altogether, so they were outnumbered—not that that mattered. They got out and spread along the sidewalk, not in any organized way, talking to each other, as if they had all the time in the world.

Everything happened slowly. At one point, a police vehicle facing the crowd snapped on its headlights, and they all lifted their hands to their eyes like those old newsreels of nuclear tests. One cop walked forward, went down on one knee in front of a seated protester, an older woman, and spoke to her privately. She had glasses and wore an oversized T-shirt with a logo I couldn't see. She must have been cold. No way she expected this to run so late. After a minute, the cop stood and extended one hand behind him, without looking, until into it some other, lesser officer placed a small, battery-operated bullhorn. Then, with a show of gallantry, the cop did something unexpected: he handed the bullhorn to the woman in the T-shirt. I could see him showing her how to use it. The woman nodded, turned her back to him, and began speaking.

"Those of us who want to go now, can go," she said. "Those of us who remain will be arrested. If you choose to be arrested, please do not resist. They brought all their expensive military cop shit out here because they want to use it. We can't give them a reason."

She handed the bullhorn back to the cop, who then took her hand and helped her to her feet.

I only saw two people, a couple, take the opportunity to leave. The floodlights on top of the vans kept the faces of the cops themselves in a kind of fractured darkness, different planes, different features suddenly visible whenever they turned their heads to speak to one another. They did their work methodically, but their impatience began to show in their movements, their expressions. They spoke very little. It seemed likely, though I hadn't heard anyone say so, that this had all been worked out in advance between the police and the protest's organizers, in an effort to avoid violence. Most of the protesters went very quietly, allowing themselves to be pulled to their feet once handcuffed, walking slowly toward one of the idling police vans. A few of them—older men and women—went limp, something you really have to be trained how to do correctly, and in those instances the officer involved would signal behind him or her and two or three more officers would help carry that protester back to the vans, carefully but dispassionately, like a corpse. My feelings began to change.

What were these people really doing here? They were not an inexhaustible resource; soon they would be gone, and the family and the landlord and the immigration agents would all still be there, and the eviction would take place. And they all knew that. True, they were making a little extra work for the cops, which annoyed them for sure, although they were probably all getting overtime to soften the blow. "Well, at least we did something," everyone would feel afterward, when in practical terms they had done nothing, except to show themselves something about themselves that they wanted to see. If I were inside that house, I might have resented them for staging this fake reprieve, for delaying the execution just so that they might later tell themselves a story about how they'd done everything they could.

"Move along, please," someone said suddenly, very close to my ear. I certainly wasn't doing anything illegal; there was no way to mistake me for part of the protest itself. Trying to tamp down my general agitation, in order not to overreact, I forced a smile and turned to look into the officer's face, and I recognized it.

It was the red-haired cop from downtown, the one who had rousted me off the public bench, the one to whom I'd so stupidly mouthed off in my outrage that I'd almost blown everything. All the features of his face—lips, skin, eyelashes— were monochrome. His mouth was set in a tense line. There's no way, I thought, no way he'd recognize me, his whole workday is made up of encounters like that; he never really saw me in the first place. But then his eyes, which had been unfocused by boredom and impatience, locked on to mine. It's possible I'd made some kind of involuntary sound.

I can't really account for my reaction. I feared and I hated him so much. His physical ugliness seemed itself like a form of sadism; the fact that I could feel such irrepressible terror in the presence of such a worthless human being made me feel ashamed. I looked at his holstered gun, looked right at it, and imagined making a lunge for it.

"Press," I said hoarsely.

He looked at me in amazement. "Don't make me laugh," he said. "I told you, move on. You can't stay here. I won't tell you again."

"This is a public street," I said, "and I am standing on it."

Some other version, some other iteration of me was standing beside me as this encounter took place, whispering in my ear: *What are you doing?* But I couldn't stop myself. He took half a step closer to me, and suddenly ran his gaze over my body and my hands. "If you're in possession of a phone or any other sort of recording device—"

"I'm not. I'm not doing anything illegal. I'm just here."

The anger in him, the indignation that I should add to his responsibilities in this way. I could feel him trembling. He seemed provoked by my looking at him, but I was unable to turn my eyes away. "What the exact fuck is your problem, sir?" he said. "Do I know you or something?"

Others were staring at us now. All the ambient noise switched off.

"Sir, turn around and put your hands behind your back," the officer said.

I smiled at him—I smiled at him!—and with a clear but uncertain path to my left, into darkness, I took off running. "No!" shouted a woman's voice behind me. The voice of one of the organizers. She wasn't worried about what would happen to me; she was worried what would happen to the rest of them, now that the contract had been broken and its terms no longer applied.

It did seem conceivable that he would let me go, that processing the other twenty or thirty demonstrators in as short a time as possible and clocking out and going home would be more appealing to him than chasing down one random panicky guy. Why go to the trouble? But I could hear him behind me. I had a decent head start, but I don't run that well, even on full adrenaline. And he was a much younger man.

It seemed ominous that he didn't say a word, didn't call out "Halt!" or anything conventional like that. Just his footsteps and his breathing. I guess it's true he didn't need to identify himself to me at that point. I was doing him a favor by taking this encounter away from others' eyes. The intersection I was headed toward was bright and the traffic pretty steady. On my left I saw a gap between two houses that looked like an alley. And it was just that: a narrow, roughly paved passage stippled with garbage cans, dark and filthy but with a light at the end, a light that was just another street to run down before I lost my wind entirely but that seemed, as it came into focus, like a practical goal. I never reached it.

He didn't grab me and stop; when he caught up to me he launched forward onto my back and brought me down, holding my arms by the biceps so that I could not protect my face from hitting the pavement. I felt the skin tear on my cheek. His full weight came down on me, like someone setting out on a surfboard, and my lungs deflated. He rested on me, casually, until he'd caught his breath, while I gasped.

"That wasn't smart," he said, and when I heard the calm in his voice, the patience and lack of irritation, I knew I was in trouble.

"I'm sorry," I said.

"And I mean you have the look of a somewhat smart guy. What's your name?"

"Really, I'm so sorry, I just panicked, you don't need—"

He took a hank of my hair in his fingers and bounced my head off the macadam. I saw a kind of white flash and then the sting of some kind of gravel or glass sticking to my forehead. "I asked you a question," he said softly, in my ear.

"I'm sorry," I said. "I apologize, I didn't mean to, you were just doing your job. I'm so sorry."

He patted down my front and back pants pockets. "No wallet, even," he said. He pushed himself off of me and slowly got to his feet. I started to do the same.

"Nope," he said. He put his foot between my shoulder blades and stomped, so that I lay flat again. "You can stay put." And as I lay there petrified, I felt a sort of disturbance in the air that turned out to be him winding up and kicking me just under the ribcage, as hard, I imagine, as he could.

"What did you say your name was?" he said. I couldn't have answered him at that point if I wanted to. I waited for the pain to subside so I could tell him; because a fingerprint was as good as a name anyway, so it would be all over soon, and in the meantime I just needed to make this stop. I would give him whatever he wanted.

"Don't worry, I'm not going to arrest you," he said. "I just want to have something to call you, while we have this conversation. Less impersonal that way."

My cheek felt like it might stick to the pavement if I tried to lift it. "Do you," I said, and then I had to stop until I could try again. He squatted down in order to hear me. "Do you remember me?"

My eyes were closed, so I only had the tone of his voice to go on. "Sure," he said. "Oh yeah. Absolutely I remember you. You're a very memorable man."

He kicked me again in the kidney area. I curled up around his foot.

"Why the fuck would I have any idea who you are? But I'll remember you now, that's for sure. You better stay out of sight because if I get bored someday when I have nothing else going on, I might even have a look around for you. Now I have one more question for you."

He pulled something off his belt. His radio crackled softly.

"What's my name?" he said.

"I don't know," I whispered, which was not the truth, I'd seen his name on his badge.

He brought down some kind of baton across the backs of my knees. It didn't feel heavy, but light, whippy, like a car antenna. I felt something there give way.

"Quiet," he said. "Decent people are sleeping. Now, what's my name?"

He put his foot on the back of my head and pressed down. I could feel the tears squeezing out of my eyes. "You don't have a name," I said.

"That is correct. Now, count to a thousand. And congratulations on your escape." I didn't count, but I waited. I don't know how long. I wasn't sure about standing, about how that would go. I moved forward on my stomach. I reached into my pocket and then blindly through the dark, grass-softened edges of the alley until, miraculously, I found my keys.

I was maybe fifteen blocks from home, but I didn't know which route to take. They all seemed obvious and fraught. It wasn't all that late—ten p.m. I guessed. I was not thinking clearly. I had to stop every half a block or so; if I got at all winded, the pain of breathing hard could not be borne. It took me an hour to get back to Sugar Street. I'm guessing an hour. It could have been much longer.

I tried to stay out of sight. My knee felt like a screw or rivet had fallen out of it: if I didn't step carefully, I could feel the whole structure start to collapse. My face and hands and arms were roughly abraded. But even apart from the physical pain, which, when it's bad, does tend to claim one's concentration, I felt ashamed.

Because he was right about me. He was right to beat me in an alley and treat me with scorn. He'd shown me who I am. If he'd had the least interest, I would have confessed everything, I would have identified myself fully, in order to make the pain stop, the fear. I had failed a test, failed every section of it, and that understanding of my own systemic weakness was not something I was going to be able to outrun or unsee. I would carry that truth inside me, and I knew I could not stand it. Nothing could erase it; I could never go back to not knowing it. At the same time, though, I was very focused on wanting to kill him. I wanted that more than I've ever wanted anything in my whole life. All the lust for violence latent in me, versus all that I would have done—would still do—to spare myself: the contradiction was laughable, and that's who I was.

I turned the corner onto Sugar Street. So many of the streetlights were broken that the light itself was not continuous but fell in pools; it was easy to stay out of them. At this point I was looking mostly down at my feet, out of exhaustion, like someone relearning how to walk. I lifted my head to see if Autumn's lights were on. In the driveway, taking up most of what would have been my passage from the street to the staircase leading to my door, was a police car.

I had thoughts of hiding far away. I knew from my wanderings some of the places where the homeless generally congregated, the underpass by the fairgrounds, the invisible-from-the-street vacant lot a few doors down from the downtown Catholic Charities building—but I didn't have the physical strength. All I could do was find the closest place to get out of sight. Once I fell asleep, there's no telling how long I'd be out, and I couldn't risk anyone with a cell phone delivering me back into the hands of the cops. Nothing near a business, nothing residential either. I willed myself to the park. There would be joggers on the path not long after dawn, so I needed to get as deep into the thin woods as I could. It was hard to gauge, in the darkness, when and where I was concealed enough to be out of sight when the light came. I probably overdid it. The branches scratched my hands and forearms, held blindly up in front of my face. The ground beneath the trees was mossy and soft. Things crawling on me, probably, but the pain left me numb to finer sensations like that.

I slept deeply but not that long. Only one of my eyes would open at first; the light filtered through the brush, and I saw that for all my disoriented attempts to push farther into the woods, I was easily visible from the open grass twenty or thirty feet away, had anyone happened by. Leaves and dirt were stuck to the wounds on my face. I had to take shallow breaths. I reached down and confirmed with my fingers that one of my knees was now significantly larger than the other.

I emerged from the trees. It would have been hard to go unnoticed, looking like I must have looked, but no one was there; no one was anywhere in sight. I limped, or staggered I suppose, out of the park. I kept to the edge of the street rather than the sidewalk, thinking that anyone who saw me in that state coming too close to their house would be tempted to call the authorities, whether out of pity or fear, no difference in terms of its consequence for me.

The sun stung my eyes. Cautiously, I made it to Sugar Street and peered down the block. The driveway was empty; the cop car was gone. If Autumn was home, she would be sleeping. My little room, my cell, my futon on the floor, my running water, presented itself as a kind of oasis in my mind. No first aid or anything of that nature—I didn't own anything like that, not even a Band-Aid—which was unfortunate. But maybe later, at a considerate hour, I could impose on Autumn for that.

Though I was in a hurry, I went up the stairs slowly, first the leg with the good knee and then the other one. That was okay; I was trying to move quietly to avoid waking Autumn anyway. I saw my hand and its skinless knuckles gripping the rail; I felt my other hand reach into my pocket and close around the key. I looked and smelled, I imagine, very much like a man who had spent the night sleeping in the dirt. There was a kind of shadow or light on the landing, just a flicker, something unfamiliar. I took another step up, gingerly shielding my eyes from the sun with a hand to my forehead, and I saw that the door to my room was broken open.

From the splintered doorway I could easily take in the whole space, and nothing was disturbed. The camp chair sat where it sat, the curtains hung still in the closed window.

There was a small stack of books, as neat as I had left it. My folded clothes sat on the floor in two unsteady piles. As quickly as I could, which was not very quickly at all, I lowered myself onto my stomach, wriggled forward a few inches, and stuck my arm underneath the futon. The envelope was gone.

S LOWLY, painfully, I struggled back to my feet. I stood in the long trapezoid of morning light that came through my front window. So this was freedom: your worst fear realized. I don't know how long I was there, but when I snapped out of it, the sunlight on the floorboards wasn't under my feet anymore.

The thinking would have to come later. I went carefully down the exterior stairs, around the corner to Autumn's front door, and knocked. It was still probably too early for her to be up; but just as I lifted my fist to knock a second time, a little louder, she opened the door.

"Jesus Christ," she said. "What the fuck! Holy shit. Get in here."

It took me a second to realize she was talking about my face. I still hadn't seen it. I stepped across the threshold, and she banged the door shut behind me as if worried someone was watching. She turned and left the room without a word, leaving me standing there, unsure if I was to follow her, suddenly desperate just to sit down; a few moments later she came back carrying a lidless shoebox in her hand.

"Come here," she said. "Come here. Can you understand me? Do you have a fucking concussion or something? Come on. In here."

I followed her into her bedroom. The bed was king-sized, unmade, with clothes and magazines pushed to one side of the mattress. It took up most of the width of the room; in the swales between the bed and the walls were what looked like more clothes. The good-sized window at the head of the bed was covered by both blackout shades and curtains, so it was pretty much pitch-dark in there. Much more soothing than the sunlight. My right eye was completely closed.

"You've got shit in your face," she said. "What is that, dirt? Jesus. Okay, sorry, I'm going to have to turn a light on," and she did. Her expression was calm, and I saw that she had makeup on. So she must have been up for a while. Her tone of voice was not worried or frightened or even especially concerned. Unfazed, I would say. It calmed me.

She took out a pair of what looked like surgical tweezers and some antiseptic wipes that she ripped open, in a practiced way, with her teeth. "This'll hurt," she said.

But I honestly didn't feel a thing. "You're not a nurse, right?" I said. "What are you?"

"Don't talk," she said. I watched through one eye as she cleaned my abraded face for a while. Her expression was still my only mirror and it didn't give much away. "I've been waiting for this day," she said, in a voice both maternal and annoyed. "I've been waiting for this day since you first showed up here. So who did this to you?"

"The cops," I said. "A cop."

"Local cop? Or somebody who came looking for you?"

"Local." That was explanation enough, apparently. She had no follow-up questions. But I did. "The cops were here last night," I said. "I saw the car. Why? Were they looking for me?"

She shook her head, concentrating. "I called them."

I felt dizzy. Kneeling in front of me, she dropped the tweezers into the shoebox and rooted around in there for something else. "You called them?" I said. "Why?"

"Because someone broke into your room. You saw that, right? Did you even go upstairs yet? Somebody broke the door in. I was outside yesterday and saw your door standing open, and I went up there calling your name, and I could see the doorframe was split. No sign of you. So I called the cops. Have you been up there?"

Our faces, as we had this conversation, were just a couple of inches apart, closer, I'm sure, than they had ever been before. Close enough to kiss, close enough for me to grab her and fall back on the bed. Close enough to reach out and put my hands around her neck. Her expression was completely neutral, nonreactive, as if she were looking up close at a picture of my face and not the face itself. "Yes," I said. "I've been up there. I've been up there for hours I think."

"And? Did they take anything? Is anything missing?"

Maybe I was too close to her, so that any movement looked outsized, like a smirk or a wink instead of just a natural twitch. But I felt right then like Autumn knew everything, like her expressionlessness was some kind of dare or taunt. Like the money was all still somewhere inside our house.

"No," I said. "Nothing's missing. Everything's still there."

She told me if I wanted any better care, I would need to go to a doctor, and when I said no, no doctors, she said yeah I figured. She said, you want a glass of water or something? I think I even have a straw, and I said yes, thanks, that'd be great, and when she left the bedroom I let myself fall from my sitting position back onto the bed, and that's the last thing I remember for a while.

How would she have known, though, that that night would have been the night to break in, the night I would be out for hours, would not return home at all? It's rare that I go out anywhere at night. I don't think she knew about the money in the envelope. That would have been just a guess, not even a highly educated one. She knows I'm not working and paying the rent six months at a time, so she could reasonably deduce that there was cash up in there somewhere. But how did she hit upon last night? Or two nights ago, or three, whatever it was. Who tipped her off?

Maybe nobody. Maybe the whole FIGHT thing was a setup; maybe it was Autumn herself who slipped the flyer under my door. I don't mean that the protest was a fake, of course, nor the organization itself. But maybe she took advantage. Maybe she took a chance that a bleeding heart like me would be interested, that I'd go, and when I left the house she was watching me and made her move.

Maybe the cop car was in her driveway because she and the cop are friends. Maybe she agreed to cut him in. Or maybe the cop did come looking for me, and that's what made her realize that this was her chance. Is she strong enough to kick that door in? It would take a few tries, loud tries, visible to neighbors. But that wouldn't necessarily be the strangest thing they've ever seen her do.

Or maybe it was a legit break-in. Maybe it wasn't her. Oscar's seen my place. There's something off, affected, about that guy. The boy, Haji, he certainly knows where I live, and the other boy, his friend with the haircut, I gave him a lot of my money but it wouldn't be a big leap for him to figure I probably didn't give him all of it. Or else he told the story to someone smarter who made that leap, Haji or someone else. Or it could just be a random burglary, the luckiest day of that burglar's life, a smelly, underfurnished, dank room with an envelope in it containing more than a hundred and fifty thousand dollars in cash.

It all amounts to the same thing. Or no, it doesn't, because any scenario involving Autumn herself means that there's a good chance the money is still nearby. That would be one way to explain why she is so solicitous now, why she, who so values her privacy, is suddenly keeping me so close.

I hear her in the kitchen when I wake up at one point. I find her bathroom, and even with the light off I get some hard news when I pass by the mirror. My face hasn't started to scab yet. My rent is paid for the next two months, and upstairs I have some clothes and a cupboard full of soup and ramen and some candy bars in the useless freezer. This is the sum of me. This is who I traveled all this way to become, and so you'd think this face in the mirror would produce in me a kind of sigh of acknowledgment, but no, I do not recognize myself at all.

So, she is capable of pity, but it is a cold, businesslike sort of pity, almost with an element of impatience to it, like, look what your inability to take care of yourself is making me do. "Your clothes still have blood on them," she says. "If you want, I can go upstairs and find something else for you to wear."

No, thanks, that's okay, I'll do it.

Getting up that flight of stairs is brutal. My ribs, my knee. Nothing in there looks the same, though everything is untouched. Because the broken door will not shut properly, some newspapers have been blown around by the wind, that's all. It's almost unbearable to be in that room. Nowhere in it to escape the feeling of being watched. I change into different clothes and go back downstairs; Autumn does not seem at all surprised by my return. "I changed the sheets, too," she says, "because yikes."

Maybe I did have a concussion. I try to think through what is happening to me, what has happened to me, but there's a kind of fog I have to fight through, and I keep falling asleep. She must go out, though I never hear her leave nor come back in. Her expression, when she looks at me, is not soft; it is detached, objective, which I guess is soft compared to how she used to look at me.

And there is a tenderness behind it. At least I think so. Either that or a barely concealed contempt, the look of someone trying to affect somberness in order not to burst out laughing. Either she is allowing herself to be tender toward me because she sees how broken and helpless I am or she is enjoying the hell out of having made a fool of me, treating me like a baby even as she makes plans for her own future based on her now possessing everything that used to be mine.

I walk into the kitchen to see what time it is, and she points proudly to two white grease-stained bags on the table from Chick-fil-A.

I don't have any pain medication, so I drink when she offers it to me. I stay mostly in the darkened bedroom, so between the drinking and the sleeping I am not always confident I know what time it is, or what day. It is hard, despite her admonishments, to keep from touching my wounds.

She's in the room, in the dark; she hears me stir and whispers, "Just getting something I need, go back to sleep." Sometime later, I open my eyes and roll onto my side and I can see, in the dark, the outline of her body in the bed, on top of the covers, facing away from me.

I HAVE VERY LITTLE TIME left now. I don't have the patience to wait until my appearance is less alarming. I put on some clean clothes at least—most of my clothes are downstairs in Autumn's bedroom now—and walk stiffly to the library. I draw stares along the way. I draw stares from a mother and her child when I pass them in the foyer. I don't care. It's a hundred to one shot that Oscar will be there—I don't even really know whether it's morning or afternoon—but there he is. He stands up when he sees me heading toward him.

"What happened to you?" he whispers.

His compassion makes me furious. I have no plan here beyond thinking he might give something away if I approach him threateningly enough. "You don't know," I say.

The librarian is already afoot, heading around her desk and in my direction.

"Know what?" Oscar says. He doesn't look all that concerned for me; his eyes are darting all around him. I have become an incriminating figure, the opposite of invisible. The lank-haired librarian is almost upon us. What a character she is. Authoritarian to her core. What is she protecting, exactly? What is she enforcing? Her life is a child's life, a little fake kingdom defended by crossed arms from reality of any kind.

"Outside," Oscar says to me and nudges my shoulder. When we are out in the sunlight, by the glassed-in community message board, he puts his hands to his forehead. "What are you trying to do, get me banned out of there?"

"You've been to my room," I say. "You've seen it. You know where it is."

"So? I didn't say nothing to her."

"I need the money. I recognize now that I don't need all of the money. But I can't have nothing. You know what will happen to me. Wait, what did you say?"

"Boy, make some sense. I don't know what kind of trouble you're in, but I'm the one Black guy you know and now I stole some money from you? Who put that beating on you? It couldn't have been that little wisp of a thing."

"What fucking wisp? What are you talking about?"

"Look," he says. "I don't know what kind of shit you're into, and I don't care, I truly don't. Somebody was around here asking about you. Some woman."

"What? When was this?"

"A week ago? I don't know. I figured out the person she was looking for was probably you. She showed me a picture. But I didn't tell her shit. Now you raving something about money, it makes a little more sense."

"What did she look like? Kind of tanned, stocky, halter top, hair piled up on her head?"

"Nope," Oscar said and narrowed his eyes. "How many women you got out looking for you? No, this was some tiny woman, young. Tattoos all down the arms like white girls do nowadays. Acted all official. Too little to bust you up like this, though. Who did that?"

"A cop," I say. "Wait. When was this?"

"I don't know, week or two ago. I didn't write it in my damn diary. Listen, you should get out of here. I'm starting to be sorry I ever talked to you." He turns to go back inside.

"Listen to me," I say. It's an act, but it's also not; everything I need to feel in this moment is available to me. "Someone took something that belongs to me, something very valuable. If I find out you had anything to do with it and didn't take this one chance to make it right with me, I will kill you."

And he laughs. He doesn't believe it even for a second. "Please, motherfucker," he says. "You're killing me right now."

Who would be looking for me? Asking about me? Who would even know to try the library? Who would have a picture of me? Was it a recent one or an old one? I should have asked Oscar that, but I didn't, and now the opportunity is gone. The question of what has been done to me may go deeper than I imagined.

I do spend some time upstairs in my violated room. Some nights, even. The door won't lock, but it will stay shut if I push the garbage can in front of it. I eat what little food is there, slowly. The food is now what the money used to be: zero sum. Whatever I use, I have no means of replacing it.

Partly for that reason, I gravitate back downstairs to Autumn's, and she never seems surprised to see me. She brings home a lot of takeout food. She never asks me to contribute, but then I'm not always sure she's buying for two. I eat what she doesn't finish. Sometimes we watch television. I couldn't tell you what's on; it's just something we sit in front of. She pours us both a drink and leaves the bottle between the glasses.

When she is asleep, I will sometimes get up to use the bathroom and then make my way as quietly as I can around the dark first floor, trying drawers, trying closets and cupboards. Some of them are locked. Left open, predictably, is the drawer in the kitchen that contains, among decks of playing cards and loose batteries and other junk, the gun. I take it out and hold it, waving it carefully but loosely in the air, getting the feel of it. It is heavy. I feel sure it's loaded, though I don't even know how to check. Gently, with the barrel facing away from me, I put it back and shut the drawer and return to bed.

THERE'S THINGS in me I don't talk about, and then there's things in me I don't know about. We're moving into that latter realm now. Truths will be revealed. Desperation is here. Hunger, fear, things like that, things I've never had to face before, not in this open-ended way. There's also a powerful—an undismissible—longing for revenge, well beyond the reach of reason. These pressures, every waking moment. My life has dropped the veil and turned to face me. I'm going to learn some things.

The first time we had sex, she was smirking, like finally she'd gotten me to confess something. Finally, I'd stopped pretending. Though not reluctant, she was strangely passive, making me do everything, take off all her clothes, pull her up from the couch, guide her in front of me into the bedroom. I felt her whole history with men in her demeanor, warped but triumphant, interested only in power, the power of choosing to whom she would grant access to herself and to whom she would not. I took her hair down. In the dark her tattoos were just shadows. I devoted myself to wiping that smirk off her face, and in the end, I did it.

The first-floor view of the kids passing by on their way to school is not as clear, and also noisier. Haji is there every day. His friend with the haircut has never reappeared, a fact I now look at in a different light.

So I have to figure out how to get Haji alone. I could of course just go out to the sidewalk and ask to speak to him, but his crew will stay right there while I do it, and in that situation he will never be honest, never feel afraid enough to be honest. There's really only one way to go about it.

I go back upstairs for the first time in a few days and the room looks different. Things have been disturbed. Maybe just by the wind but I don't think so.

Odd that she still hasn't asked me about repairing my broken door, nor made any move toward hiring anyone to do it. Most likely she doesn't think about it at all; she has forgotten this part of her house even exists. She's got a strange sort of shine to her eyes these days. Maybe she is taking something. She goes out for only an hour or two most days, some days not at all. I don't believe she enjoys fucking me in a physical sense, but it makes her feel wanted, and she starts to act sullen and mean if that want is too long in manifesting. I've got fantasies that jumpstart me, that keep me going. Not the sort I can share with her. I fantasize about holding a gun to her head as she kneels in front of me and asking her where my money is.

I'm pouring some flat soda down the kitchen drain when I hear the sound of movement behind me. I yank open the

drawer and pull out a dull knife and spin around in a crouch
to face the room, and there is a fucking squirrel in there.

It seems possible that she might one day out of nowhere
disappear again, or lock her door and refuse to let me back
in. If that happened, I'd still have access to my room upstairs
as a way of avoiding the elements. Food enough for a couple
of days or a week. I am starting to game these matters out.

The fact that she doesn't ask me to contribute in terms
of food or liquor must mean she understands I have no money
now. Which must mean she knows what happened to it. Of
course I think it was most likely her, but I have to be careful,
I have to eliminate the other possibilities first, because the
moment I confront her, it's over, she will put me out on the
street whether I'm right or wrong.

My rent is paid up for another twenty-five days, if that
still means anything. She may have forgotten all about that.
I did have to remind her last time. Just in terms of my own
stability, I'm not sure whether it's better to think about dead-
lines or not.

Sitting on her blanket-covered couch while she is out,
picking up her check she says, I hear a knocking sound. It
comes again—patient and regular, not loud—and I realize
that it is the sound of someone knocking on my broken
front door upstairs. Instinctively, I duck below the level
of the couch back. I hear soft, slow steps. When I decide
it's safe to raise my head and look out the front window, I

see a woman—short, not much more than five feet, with short hair and numerous earrings, wearing a dress and a jean jacket—standing on the sidewalk with her back to me, intently reading something on her phone. After half a minute she puts the phone back in her shoulder bag, lifts her face (which I still can't see) appreciatively toward the sun, and disappears down Sugar Street.

"I could try to find work," I say idly one night when we're sitting outside on the front step. Autumn snorts. "Doing what?" she says. "Not whatever it was you did before." Across the street from us is an open garage door out of which music blares. It keeps our remarks to each other short and loud.

The city election has come and gone; all the little yard signs are gone, too, with one exception, that billboard-looking military shot of Judge Hubert. Too heavy to move easily, I guess: probably a two-person job. Or maybe this was the plan all along, to leave his avatars all around the city, smiling, watching. The view of the sign is much different down here on the first floor. It keeps catching me by surprise, I keep thinking there is some guy standing across the street with a helmet under his arm.

Autumn says she has a doctor's appointment, so I have a couple of afternoon hours alone. Today, then, is the day. The Wysocki kids pass by in front of her window, left to right, boisterous, unhurried. When the group moves on and the noise dies down, I go out to the street, turn right, and follow them.

I maintain a gap of about fifty yards, trying to look up only when necessary. Haji—wearing a polo shirt, a new-looking one, and cuffed jean shorts and high-tops—is listening to music on cordless headphones, staying with the group but in his own world. It's not hard to imagine him pointing to my window and telling his friend there's a crazy white man up there who's an easy mark or that he's the one who suggested the candy scam in the first place. At a minimum, he knows that friend's name.

I have to pay attention, because I have no idea which is his stop, so to speak. We turn off Sugar at Walnut and then off Walnut at Grove. No one appears to have noticed me, even in my state. But kids are not attentive. Everything inside their world is so unbearably important and intense that even things on the edge of their vision might as well not exist. Suddenly, Haji turns and heads up a stoop, and another boy enters the house with him.

I stop and wait until the rest of the group is out of sight. Then I advance. The house is white with gray shutters, none of the paint recent, and from my angle it has a slight rightward lean to it. One of the street-facing windows is covered with newspaper. But I don't have time for these details. All that matters to me now is the unseen. I walk up the steps and knock nonofficiously on the door.

The other, younger boy answers. "Could I please speak to Haji?" I say. "It's okay, he knows me."

Based on the boy's expression he does not accept the premise that it is okay. He shuts the door gently in my face, and I am not sure what this signifies. I settle on taking a few steps back, down the stairs, so that I might be seen from the windows and judged too poorly dressed to be a representative of the government or law enforcement. A few seconds later, the front door opens again, slowly, cautiously; Haji stands in the opening, blocking it, one hand on the jamb and the other on the door frame. "What you want?" he says.

From my position halfway down the steps he appears about a foot and a half taller than me. But he is not a threat to me, not really; it will always be the other way around. I see a curtain move and another face appears in a first-floor window, another boy, this one maybe six or seven years old.

I have no plan. I suppose my plan was that the sight of me would cause him to panic and confess, that if my expression suggested that I knew everything already, he would come clean out of self-interest. But that isn't what's happening. I don't know everything; in fact I know nothing at all. That's probably what is written on my face, whatever I intend.

"Do you remember me, Haji?" I say.

His chin pulls back slightly when I say his name; he instantly loses a little bit of his bluster, and from this I can tell that he does not recognize me, that he is frightened and undermined the way anyone would be if a total stranger suddenly addressed you by name. He has been on the threshold of my home, and he has spoken to me at least twice, but he has no memory of any of this. Of course I do look a little different now, probably alarmingly so.

"What you want?" he says again.

"I want," I say, "my money."

A true statement, whether he has it or not.

Next door, a man leans out of his window.

Haji looks back over his shoulder and shakes his head. "You crazy?" he says to me.

"You sold me candy," I say—a little louder now, since others, visible and invisible, are listening. "You came to my home. Your friend with the fade, he came there too. I gave you money. I gave him money. And now it's gone."

Now he is afraid. He shakes his head again, at me. "No," he said. "What are you doing? Who are you?"

"Where's my money?" I say.

A voice inside me is trying to settle me. Speaking low and nonstop, it is saying: Obviously he doesn't have it, does he look like someone who just came into a hundred and fifty thousand dollars, what, do you think he invested it? And look at his face. Look at it. He obviously has no idea what you're talking about. Kids are good liars but you can still tell the truth from an act, can't you? And what if he does have it? What if he does have it? What were you going to do with it anyway, except use it to extend your claim on your own worthless life? What would he do with it, if he had it? And how did you get it in the first place, what, that just doesn't matter anymore?

But no logic can reach me now, not even my own; all of that is no match for what's on the surface of me, for the part of me that faces and meets the world. "You know what happened!" I yell. "Tell me! Tell me and I'll let you go!"

He steps back and closes the door.

The man leaning out his window is gone now, too, but I still feel surveilled. I'm alone in the street, maybe four in the afternoon, and it's impossible to tell whether the sense that I'm in danger is coming from within me or from the air. I run from it, not very gracefully or well, but I run until I'm out of breath and can look behind at the empty street to see that no one is pursuing me.

JULY 1 comes and goes. No mention from Autumn of the rent. I still have some winter clothing upstairs, but everything else has made the transition to her place. It's all on the floor; she's never mentioned clearing a drawer for me or anything like that. I try to keep the piles neat.

If she has my money, then it's not inconceivable that she considers my rent, so to speak, already paid, and I am good to stay here indefinitely. So long as the status quo is that I am completely, entirely dependent on her, she seems okay with it. I still search the place when she's out. Sometimes I want to challenge her directly, but the level of risk there is still too high. I have nowhere else to go.

We have less sex now than we used to; on that score, I guess she feels her point has been made.

The Judge Hubert sign, incredibly, is still out there, its frame held down by sandbags. I wish I still had Oscar's saw. There he stands, fit and smug in his desert camo, briefly emerged from the turret of his tank. You know, for Justice. Apparently he came back from a few years of murdering random brown people to protect rich white people's access to oil—excuse me, "fighting terrorism"—and his big revelation was: You know what kind of career all this arrogant, detached, technologically based racist killing has really prepared me for? The Law! And not advocacy, either, but impartiality, because who causes suffering less partially than me? Presumably white voters saw that picture of him on his tank and agreed: yes, please, let this guy keep up the good work of administering justice in some place that I will never have to see.

I have a sort of daydream in which I appear before him. It's not consistent, though, because sometimes he shoots me through the chest with some kind of missile while people cheer and other times he lets me go, just waves a hand and lets me go, after all I've done, after all my selfish transgressions and the suffering I've caused, just because, apart from the muscles maybe, I look a little like him.

Summer heat again. Autumn says she has a new front-of-house job at a tattoo parlor, keeping track of appointments, taking payments, just part-time; then she says it's not really an official job, just helping a friend of hers out of the goodness of her heart. Some or none of this may be true. When she's absent, I take the opportunity to get out of the dark apartment and breathe some air. I don't go far—just around the block once usually—because I can't lock her door.

School is out for the summer. The hotter it is, the fewer fellow pedestrians I see, but there are some. Lately I do let myself reminisce, because reminiscing is a way to hold off the future. I don't reflect on my old life, though, but on the year just past, on the way that I pontificated about making my world smaller, and now my world has shrunk to the point where the block itself is the entirety of it.

The last leg of this modest orbit puts me back on Sugar Street, tracing the path the students take to school in the morning. It's pleasantly shady and the smells are a mélange of blooming trees and household garbage. A rather petite young woman is on my side of the street, walking in the opposite direction, wearing a sundress, big sunglasses, short hair, tattooed arms, multiple and asymmetrical earrings. We have to turn sideways to avoid contact on the sidewalk as we pass, just a few feet from Autumn's driveway, and we do so with a social smile. And then, from behind me, as I turn down the driveway and approach the door, I hear my real name.

I STOP, but I don't turn around. She is certainly no one I recognize. I don't think she's come to kill me; she's not the type (though maybe that makes her perfect for the job), and here on the street in the middle of the day seems an unnecessarily reckless place for it to happen.

Still, I wait and brace myself.

"All right!" she says happily, triumphantly, like a kid. "Score! I can't believe it's finally you. You can turn around, it's okay."

I turn around, and she takes a picture of me with her phone.

"Who are you?" I say. "You're not a cop?"

"Hold on a sec . . . wait . . . and send," she says. "Sorry? No, I'm not a cop. Do I look like a cop?" She looks like a pixie. She is so small I feel that even I could take her in any sort of physical battle, and I wonder how she has accounted for that. She is still six or eight feet away from me. "I'm a private investigator," she says.

"What's your name?"

"Not really important, right?"

"Who hired you?"

191

"Well, you can probably figure that one out. Your business partner, with a big assist from your wife." Her phone pings; she suspends everything to check it, as they all do, and she barks out a laugh. "Speak of the devil," she says.

"How did you find me?"

She beams. "I was hoping you'd ask me that!" she says. "It was awesome. Nothing, nada, for like four or five months, and then your car randomly turned up in a bust in the middle of nowhere. By the time I got there, the cops had gotten the guy to flip on the salvage yard where he bought it, and they let me talk to that guy and he described the whole encounter with you. And that was just the beginning! All I had at that point was you on a county road headed east. The key to it, really, was trying to think like you, trying to figure what move a guy like you would make next, smart guy without a lot of survival skills. I thought, okay, it has to be a city . . ."

"Fine, okay, that's enough," I say. "I don't know why you're telling me all this. I don't know why you've outed yourself to me at all. Now that I know I'm found I'll just get lost again. Unless your plan is to bring me back somehow, which—"

"No, man, a bounty hunter I am not. My job was to find you, and you're found. They've got your location, a current photo. There are warrants out for your arrest, so things'll start to happen now, things that have nothing to do with me. Hey, did you know that you could be divorced in absentia? In some states anyway. I never knew that before. Anyway, congratulations, you're a single guy now." She looks at her phone again. "She's texting me like crazy," she says.

I am burning to go inside—I am making a list of next moves in my head—but it occurs to me that, though Pixie P.I. knows my address, she may not know I'm living downstairs now, and I don't want to give it away. Maybe she is trying to make me do exactly that? But no. "Go ahead," she says, and it is humiliating to be read so easily by such a person. "It's okay. I know the living situation. Autumn still claims this all happened by accident, that you just randomly showed up at her door, but I don't know if that's credible. What, did you meet her online or something? Run away to be together? Usually when guys like you pull that, the woman on the other end is like nineteen. So, you know, kudos I guess?"

"You talked to her?" I say. "To Autumn?"

"Yeah, just like an hour or two ago. Met her for coffee, told her everything. Corrected her impressions. If I were you I would buy her some flowers or something, dude."

I turn my back to her again and try not to run toward the house. I'm struck by the fact that she hasn't asked me about the money. Opening the door, I look over my shoulder; once again I am looking at the back of her head, as she takes a selfie with the house and myself in the background.

Time is no longer money; time is time. When I'm sure the detective is gone, I exit Autumn's and go up the side stairs to my room. The windows haven't been opened in a while.

There is nothing there I want to take, and nothing, in any case, to put it in, since the various gym bags and boxes in which I traveled across the country were all thrown away a year ago. Hardly anything in the place but its surfaces, and those surfaces are now all evidence. Traces of me must be everywhere. It couldn't be otherwise. I am hit forcefully by what seems like a great and necessary idea, which is to set fire to the house. Autumn has matches downstairs someplace. But you don't burn down a house with a book of matches. The futon doesn't even look flammable; they probably make them nowadays with that in mind. I don't have time to figure it out. I head back down the stairs, leaving the door open behind me, and halfway down I think of something: Maybe it was the detective who broke into my room. Maybe the reason she didn't ask about the money is that she already has the money. Maybe it's purely about revenge now, about punishment, judgment. Well, I will not be judged.

Under Autumn's sink I find some kind of tote bag. I go into the bedroom and jam as many items of my clothing inside it as I can. Then I go back to the kitchen and grab half a dozen of those power bars she eats and stuff those in there too. What I need most is money, but I've looked everywhere for it. I look again anyway. I slide the mattress off the frame, I pull down whatever crap is on the shelf in her closet, and when I hear footsteps, Autumn's footsteps, in the driveway, I run to the kitchen, open the junk drawer, grab the gun, and lay it gently in the tote bag with a shirt folded over it.

"Good, you're packed. I was hoping you'd be gone already. I know you like to run out on people without saying anything, but I guess on top of everything else that sucks about you, you're too fucking slow.

"I had the idea there was something different about you. I don't know why. I had the idea that you were genuinely fucked up in some interesting way. But you're boring as fucking hell. You're just as boring as you look. Why didn't I trust that? Why did I think in your case appearances were deceiving? Appearances are never fucking deceiving. You're just another one. You're just like all of them. You're totally ordinary, another guy who gets older and gets bored and cuts out on his family and lets them fend for their fucking selves. Oh yeah. I know. I know it all now. Some little bitch tells me she's got some information about the guy living with me and I get all excited, thinking now I'm finally going to get the real story. And I do get the real story, and it's boring as hell, and do you know why? Because I've known asshole men like you my entire fucking life. It's been a parade of men exactly like you. Mr. Outlaw, Mr. Off the Grid. Please.

"Your wife never wants to see you again, by the way, if you're wondering. Your partner never wants to see you again. They just want you to not get away with it. And that's what I want, too, for you to not get away with it, because guys like you get away with everything, all your fucking lives. I've seen a lot of shit in my life, I've survived a lot of asshole men, and at this point I kind of pride myself on not getting surprised again, on not getting disappointed, but let me tell you, I have never been so disappointed in my life. A travel agency? You owned a travel agency. Co-owned. And you stole all your partner's money and cleaned out your wife and ran off to live here. What a brave move. Why here? Why fucking here? That'll remain a mystery I guess. And where's that money? What happened to it? Where did it go? It must not have been much. It didn't get you very far, even living like a fucking bum. Travel agency! Where the fuck are *you* gonna go?

"Well, nothing more I can do to you now, asshole, though if I could think of anything, I'd do it. Get out. Hit the road. Kill yourself. That seems like your best move right now, frankly. I was thinking on the drive over here what I would do if I were in your spot and that's really the best I could come up with. Anyway, for fuck's sake don't do it here. Get out. Now. Now. That's it. Keep going. Don't even fucking look at me. Fuck you for ever being born, you worthless piece of shit. You want to be forgotten? Done, I just did it, I just forgot all about you, you're erased, you never fucking existed. Go!"

IN THE PARK I find the patch of woods where I spent the night after my beating. I have held a gun only once before. I figure out where the safety is and, miraculously, it's on. At length I am able after all to figure out how to eject the magazine; there are six bullets in there.

They are my assets now. The mistake I made with the money was that I waited too long and those assets were squandered. Apart from the five grand I gave to the boy: that money probably did some sort of good. Made something different, at least. The rest of my assets sat under my futon, under the literal weight of me, as I slept, where they did no good at all. Well, that's a mistake I won't make this time. My time is short, no matter how you look at it, and I won't go with any potential unspent. And this is the part where I'm supposed to say, "And the last bullet will be for me," but I actually don't think that will be necessary.

Sleeping in the park is a no go. I can't risk arrest, and also it looks like rain. Holding my tote bag with the gun in it, I make my way downtown to the Catholic Charities building. I take the least direct route possible, staying off all main streets until the end when I can't avoid it, looking around every corner for a face that would recognize mine, for the detective, or Autumn, or Oscar, Haji, the kid with the fade, the red-haired cop. When I arrive, I stand briefly in a line of men, my face turned away from the street, and I am given a slip of paper with a number on it, and that slip of paper turns into a bowl of soup and a cot in a room full of cots. I see people staring at me, at my bag. I'd stay awake all night if I could, but it's not possible, so I sleep with the tote bag in my arms.

Well, "sleep." It's in the night, of course, on my back, staring in the direction of the invisible ceiling, that the reckoning comes. My old business partner: we sat across from each other every day for fourteen years and already it is an effort to picture him. I'm sure he hates me. The business was failing anyway; the internet killed it. We were surviving by offering package ecotours to environmentally pristine places, thus contributing greatly to the defilement of said places. I tried to talk to him about that once, and he looked at me like I was insane. Our wives were better friends than we were; I wonder what that's like now.

As for my wife and I, I remember, we got along mostly by hiding our real feelings from each other. It became a form of consideration.

There is a child, too, a daughter, but she is no longer a child, and we don't know where she is. Her attitude toward us turned accusatory when she was about fifteen and never changed. I don't know if she has any idea that I'm gone, that her mother is now alone . . . I can imagine their suffering, I really can. But when I try to gin up some personal remorse over it, I feel like I'm acting, it's like being remorseful for something somebody else did. The person with whom my name and face are still associated by some: that person is dead. Their frustration is understandable, but it can't touch me now. All around me in the dark, the sounds of unconscious men.

In the morning I am asked if I would like to attend a church service. I thank the man and leave the building, and when he asks compassionately if he'll see me again that evening, I realize that he might.

Where do judges hang out? Courthouses. You don't need to be some pixie detective to figure that one out, it's just common sense. They're not always there, court's not always in session, and they don't seem in general like nine-to-five types. But if you have the time and are patient, there is no way they won't show up eventually. If they walk in, they have to walk out.

But first. A long, long hike out near the fairgrounds, not far at all from where I abandoned the car in which I arrived here a year ago. It's a beautiful day. Cloudless, not too hot. The train tracks run through these undeveloped acres, near the highway, elevated a few feet above the brackish ground. The drone of insects, the irregular, beating swoosh of fast cars displacing the air.

I have to fire the gun at least once, for practice. It's a waste of a bullet, maybe, but it will mean the second time I fire it my body will know what to expect and my aim will likely be better.

It's not long, an hour maybe, before a train approaches. I can hear the vibrations in the track itself before I can see it. It's a freight, which is lucky—slow and loud, almost no human beings on board. I stand and admire it for a while, then I turn my back to it. Shielded from sight, covered by the strained roar of the wheels bearing tons of who knows what, I lift up the gun with both hands and fire—at nothing, into the reeds. Though I have little sense of how loud it is, I can feel the recoil in both shoulders. It hurts! More importantly, I feel how that flinch from the pain lifts the barrel upward, just a touch but enough to make a difference. So it is a matter of being prepared for that and also for the fact that I will need to get up close.

I turn back to face the tracks and sit down in the grass. The gun is hot in my hand; I click the safety and lay it down behind me. The train is fantastically long; it must be ten minutes before the last car pulls the curtain of the sky across my vision. When it is quiet again—except for the insects and the cars, briefly drowned out but always there—I stand up.

M Y MANIFESTO:

Draw a tight circle around your life and let everything outside that circle fade to black. Direct physical action is what
matters. What else is there to work with? Words? Words are
useless—worse than useless, in fact, because they feed the
speaker's own vanity. And if you want to talk about money
as a way of making the world better, the only problem with
money is that the bad guys will always have more of it.

How did silence get such a bad rap? Everybody these days
thinks the world of their own voice, thinks that by raising
that voice, they're doing something. Wrong. Nobody except
you cares what you have to say. Silence does not equal com-
plicity; silence equals humility and also practicality. Silence
turns your attention away from yourself. Am I talking about
the importance of listening? Yeah, sure, a little I suppose, but
it's more inward looking, more personal than that. Just stop
talking, stop posting, stop tweeting. Shut up. A lot opens
up to you, to your mind and your senses, once you do that.

Because in the end you are not a voice. You are not a name, not an identity; all that is vanity. In the end you are a body. That is the most, maybe the only, useful thing at your disposal. You must not flatter or deceive yourself about that.

And it's harder for some than for others. It doesn't matter who I am, but here are a few demographic facts just so you know roughly where I'm coming from: I am a white man, born in the twentieth century. I am American. I am straight and was not raised in conditions of poverty. The places I lived, the schools I went to, the jobs I applied for: I never had to think about how any of those things came to be there. They were just there. As was I. No one ever had to bother to encourage me to think of myself as an individual, to think of my efforts and successes as individual efforts and successes, because I thought of them that way automatically.

But I am not an individual. My voice is a fiction and a distraction. It took me many years to realize this. It took me many years to stop cherishing myself. To some, that understanding is second nature, but for people like me, it's been difficult to acquire, because the world told me otherwise for so long.

I'm not blaming other people. I made a lot of mistakes. Mostly what I've made are mistakes. But that's why you have to do something. There's no second life where you get to apply all that you learned about yourself in the first one. You can't just keep doing the same things over and over, petering out that way, and flattering yourself that it matters a damn how you *feel* about it all.

The truth is I got tired of my history. The personal, the political, it's all one history for a guy like me: the history of hurting people without meaning to and then saying sorry. All the long-ago historical grotesquerie for which people wanted to hold me responsible: I don't mean that that presumption was unfair. I just wanted out from under it, I wanted to start over. A lot of nice liberal white men might say something similar, but so what? The point is to make it happen. Your lineage, your name, these things don't have to define you, not if you don't let them. You don't have to own what you inherit. You can begin again. You can rebrand. You can go to sea, you can light out for the territories. It's the classic American story.

My old spot in the world, by the way, was a fairly cushy one—unconsciously advantaged, privilege-derived—and now that spot is open. You're welcome.

Autumn was wrong: I am a sleeper. Was.

Also, just get off the fucking internet. Forget the idea that anything happens there. It's a playground, it's an opiate. The whole reason it exists is to ensure that nothing ever changes.

You have no purpose, no meaning. You are not "here for a reason." You do have, once you open yourself up to it, an opportunity.

You must make your life smaller, because that makes your own proportional value greater. Scale yourself up. One to one. Or, in my own best-case scenario now, one to five.

Maybe a fella ain't got a soul of his own, but only a piece of a big one.

Forget the systemic. Forget the intersectional. Just do what you can do to reduce the amount of suffering that you can see right in front of you. Not everybody's got the stomach for it, of course. We'll see if I have the stomach for it.

Nobody sees me anymore, because nobody wants to see me. I'm a down-on-his-luck white man. They want me to exit the world—both those who know me best and those who just walk past me sitting on the sidewalk, propped up against the federal building, across from the courthouse. Well, I want to exit the world, too, but it'll all feel a little less vain if I can take some people with me when I go.

My privilege is all gone, but what survives, it turns out, is the feeling of privilege—of what is due me, of how I demand to be treated—and that feeling may be reprehensible and wrong, but it can still be empowering and even useful.

Why the judge, some will ask? It makes plenty of sense when you think about it: because of the tank. Because of whatever he did when he was invisible inside that tank instead of posing on it for his portrait. Because of the suffering he has caused so many of the people who have been brought before him. Because he presumes to consider himself a judge of men at all and to ask us to consider him one. And also because I don't want to get caught. So basically, two reasons: one, because there's no connection; two, because it's all connected.

I went to the woods to live deliberately—

That's him.

The world is a ruined place, and that is our doing. Some of us much more than others. Still, it's a fantasy that you are somehow going to make this world better by adding something to it, bringing something to it. The only way to improve this world is to subtract from it. Only subtract.

In my imagination, he was walking to his car in some underground garage, me a few silent steps behind him, and we were the only two people in the picture. But there's no underground garage, just a VIP lot that's full of people, some of whom wave to him, some of whom call to him, as I start down the next rank of cars. Still, it's not impossible that I will get away with it. People are famously startled when something like this happens; their memory is famously clouded. Who could recall me? I might well walk away, my time still unexhausted.

If I don't, though, that's okay. Still a net gain for the unjudged of this world.

He turns, and in his eyes there is a flicker of acknowledgment that something may be wrong, but he still gives me a big, reflexive smile, that old campaigner. From up close he looks nothing like me at all.

GROVE PRESS

Reading Group Guide

by Paula Cooper Hughes

SUGAR STREET

Jonathan Dee

ABOUT THIS GUIDE

We hope that these discussion questions will enhance your reading group's exploration of Jonathan Dee's *Sugar Street*. They are meant to stimulate discussion, offer new viewpoints, and enrich your enjoyment of the book.

More reading group guides and additional information, including summaries, author tours, and author sites for other fine Grove Atlantic titles may be found on our website, groveatlantic.com.

QUESTIONS FOR DISCUSSION

The opening description of the American interstate highway system recalls an almost soaring era of hand-out-the-window adventure, of ecstatic physical freedom. How did you react when the narrative abruptly shifts to today's reality, that of being incessantly tracked and "your whereabouts becoming data, instantly" (p. 1)?

───────────

When the author reveals that the protagonist carries with him an envelope of possibly "ill-gotten" money, the secret of which isn't revealed until the end, what sorts of things did you speculate about how the protagonist obtained it (p. 2)?

───────────

The protagonist describes the challenge of finding a place to pull off and stop in the first part of the story, a place where someone won't call a cop because they see a car parked in a place it shouldn't be. Indeed, throughout *Sugar Street*, the juxtaposition of intimate, small-town surveillance vs. large-scale, digital-age surveillance is an ongoing theme. Are they qualitatively different in terms of the potential threat they pose to the protagonist?

───────────

The protagonist is not sugar-coated in any way. He is and was—in his previous life—a self-avowed privileged white male with all the perks and advantages that status avails him. Yet his inner thoughts paint the picture of a cowering, often angry, self-loathing victim. Does this contrast, from the perspective of any reader who isn't a white male, make you wonder if white men in general feel this way, or is he a special case? If you are a white male, did you identify with the protagonist, or did his inner musings surprise you? For all, what about him as a character did you find to be sympathetic and why?

―――――――――――

By the end of the first chapter, the protagonist has been told he looks alternately like a cop by the body work guy and a sex offender, sober alcoholic, and bomb maker by Autumn, while he fancies himself an outlaw, an antihero. What do the other characters' assessments of him reveal about them? How did seeing him through their eyes affect your ability to conjure him?

―――――――――――

The Wysocki Middle School children act as a sort of modern-day Greek chorus, reflecting racial, sexual, and ethnic tension, the sting of isolation, and the not particularly subtle threat of mob psychology. The protagonist's interest in them initially feels like casual curiosity—a way to pass the time—but becomes increasingly off-putting as he unravels. How did you read the kids' presence in the narrative and their interactions with the protagonist as you moved through the story? How do you think they helped shape the plot?

―――――――――――

While we only see the protagonist physically as "types" through others' eyes, he continually describes Autumn in minute detail as "hard looking" (p. 24)—based on her shorts, her tattoos, her tight tank tops, her directness, "like she's been put together out of mismatched parts, some kind of chop shop of physiques" (pp. 18–19)—a sort of repulsive queen. What does his impression of her reveal about him? Does it hint at her strengths or vulnerabilities? Or does his privileged white maleness skew his opinion such that it reveals nothing?

―――――――――――

The protagonist describes the internet: "All that instant connection to the world, to friends and strangers, to 'the news,' it feels like the human condition when you're in it, but when you're outside it you see that all along it was just a product, something sold to you so relentlessly every minute of every day that you forgot it was transactional at all" (p. 38). How did you react to this passage? Did it affect the way you view your life? If it did, might this perspective encourage you to change your behavior? If so, how?

———

There are many observations in *Sugar Street* that might stop readers in their tracks. How did you react to the protagonist's declaration that "if white people had a tombstone, it would read, 'They Stopped At Nothing'" (p. 49)? Do you think his views are informed by his being on the "inside" of privileged white maleness, more a sign of the times—or something else?

———

What about the protagonist's feeling that "democracy, capitalism, liberalism: [are] all in the lurid end-stages of their own failure, yet we won't even try to imagine anything different, any other principal around which life might be organized: we would sooner choke each other to death" (p. 49)? What different kinds of social constructs can you envision that would work better? What do you think it would take to achieve them? Or do you agree that humans are just too dug in to change, that we're doomed?

———

The protagonist is obsessed with avoiding being tracked or identified throughout the narrative. From a practical standpoint, he doesn't want to get caught for the crime he's committed. But from a philosophical one, his aversion goes deeper, predating and separate from his life on the lam. On page 59, he states that his "deal came down to privacy." He couldn't stand "being exposed all the time." Yet he obsessively observes and tracks every detail about the people around him, aggregating those details into presumptions about their histories. Is data collection an inescapable part of human nature, human survival? And once the right technology was introduced, did our evolutionary wiring make this hyper form of surveillance inevitable?

――――――――

The same people tend to walk by our houses every day in a neighborhood setting, something we're perhaps more aware of given the uptick in remote work. If you saw a kid that passes your house every day drop a notebook on the way home from school, would you set it aside for him or her? What do you make of Autumn's response on page 54: "Yeah," she says, "that seems totally normal." Isn't it normal? Is it just the protagonist's fugitive status that makes everything he does seem suspect? Or is this observation more a reflection of who Autumn is?

――――――――

On page 80, the protagonist declares: "Fear is humiliating, and humiliation, in its aftermath, breeds anger." How did his observation strike you? What did it illuminate about his character and others in the book?

――――――――

The issue of race and racial tension is a constant undercurrent in *Sugar Street*. Autumn unselfconsciously declares that she is renting her room to the protagonist because he is the first comer who isn't Black. The protagonist takes an interest in Abiha especially and the other mostly immigrant children generally and yet is so personally uncomfortable with Oscar, who more than once helps him out of a jam. The Yemeni house is set on fire by an arsonist, an act that is surmised to be a hate crime. These details are punctuated by intermittent letters to the editor decrying the acts of certain kinds of people without naming race or immigration status outright. How representative of your community is the racial tension described in the book? Do you think that tension has grown or waned in recent times?

———

The protagonist reflects on the house fire that killed the Yemeni adult and child and decides ultimately that the house is too far away from Wysocki Middle School for the child to have been a student there. Going further, he's bothered that it even matters to him whether she was a Wysocki student. "A girl died in her bedroom in a fire. How is that any more real if it happens to touch your own experience in some thirdhand way? Ego is all that is" (p. 87). Do you agree that "ego is all that is" or do you believe that humans are reflexively tribal?

———

During the silent vigil to protest the eviction of the nameless immigrants, the protagonist suggests that it's only so the protestors could later say, "'Well, at least we did something,' . . . when in practical terms they had done nothing, except to show themselves something about themselves that they wanted to see" (p. 155). Has protesting become performative? Is it dangerous to believe you've "done something" when you actually haven't? What kinds of modern-day protests, whether you agree ideologically or not, do you think have initiated the most positive change? What kinds of societal or political circumstances do you think might have helped catalyze that change?

———

Why do you think the protagonist and Autumn start sleeping together after the cop beat the him up? Did you view Autumn differently when she begins to take care of him? When she begins to sleep with him? Did you see him differently after he sleeps with someone whose views appear to be abhorrent to him? Or is all his liberalism just like the protesters who believe they've "done something"?

———